PUFFIN BOOKS
HOW I TAUGHT MY GRANDMOTHER
TO READ AND OTHER STORIES

Sudha Murty was born in 1950 in Shiggaon in north Karnataka.
An M.Tech. in Computer Science, she teaches Computer Science to
postgraduate students. She is also the Chairperson of the Infosys
Foundation. A prolific writer in Kannada, she has written seven
novels, four technical books, three travelogues and two collections
of short stories. Her previous English book *Wise and Otherwise*
has been translated into thirteen Indian languages. This is her first
book for children.

HOW I TAUGHT MY GRANDMOTHER
TO READ AND OTHER STORIES

SUDHA MURTY

PUFFIN BOOKS

PUFFIN BOOKS
Published by the Penguin Group
Penguin Books India Pvt. Ltd, 11 Community Centre, Panchsheel Park, New
Delhi 110 017, India
Penguin Group (USA) Inc., 375 Hudson Street, New York, New York 10014,
USA
Penguin Group (Canada), 90 Eglinton Avenue East, Suite 700, Toronto M4P
2Y3
Penguin Books Ltd, 80 Strand, London WC2R 0RL, England
Penguin Ireland, 25 St Stephen's Green, Dublin 2, Ireland (a division of Penguin
Books Ltd)
Penguin Group (Australia), 250 Camberwell Road, Camberwell, Victoria
3124, Australia (a division of Pearson Australia Group Pty Ltd)
Penguin Group (NZ), 67 Apollo Drive, Rosedale, North Shore 0632, New
Zealand (a division of Pearson New Zealand Ltd)
Penguin Group (South Africa) (Pty) Ltd, 24 Sturdee Avenue, Rosebank,
Johannesburg 2196, South Africa

Penguin Books Ltd, Registered Offices: 80 Strand, London WC2R 0RL,
England

First published in Puffin by Penguin Books India 2004

Copyright © Sudha Murty 2004

20 19 18 17 16 15

Typeset in Sabon by Mantra Virtual Services, New Delhi
Printed at Pauls Press, New Delhi

Dedicated to
the citizens of tomorrow
who will bring
changes in
our country

Contents

FOREWORD

I was brought up in a village. Those days there were no televisions, music systems or VCDs at home. Our only luxury was books. I was fortunate to have grandparents. My grandfather was a retired school teacher and an avid reader. He knew a vast number of Sanskrit texts by heart and every night, under the dark sky with the twinkling stars, he would tell me many stories. These were stories from the history of India, the epics and whatever interesting things he had read that day in the papers and magazines. These tales taught me some of my first lessons in life. The Katha Saritsagara (the Ocean of Stories), Arabian Nights, Panchatantra, stories of Aesop, Birbal and Tenali Rama were told to me during those beautiful nights.

The years rolled by, and so much changed in India. Now families are nuclear and children rarely get to live with their grandparents. The arrival of TV and the dramatizations of our ancient epics brought these stories closer to us and helped us know them, but it also removed the power of imagination. Storytelling is not easy. It requires the proper modulation of voice, in order to create an atmosphere of horror, surprise, humour or peace. During those storytelling nights, I have travelled with my grandfather to the battlefield of Haldi Ghati in Rajasthan and cried for the dead horse Chetak. I enjoyed the victory of Shivaji sitting next to his great mother Jeejabai. I have been thrilled listening to the description of the battles of Raja Ranjit Singh and moved to tears with the stories of his large-heartedness. I cried when the first war of Independence, which the British called 'Mutiny', was lost. While listening to my grandfather, in my mind I became an Arab and changed my dress to walk the streets of Baghdad and inspect the thieves with the Wazir-e-Alam. I have laughed and learnt valuable lessons about knowledge and wit from the stories of Aesop, Tenali Rama and Birbal.

In this collection, I have tried to recreate some stories from my experiences, all of which have taught me something. In the course of my work for the Infosys Foundation and as a teacher, I meet many people, young and old, each of whom has enriched my life in some way. I have always wanted to tell these stories to the next generation. I hope you will like and enjoy reading them.

I want to thank Sudeshna Shome Ghosh of Penguin India. Had she not insisted, the stories would have remained in my mind for ever.

I would like to add that the royalty of this book is donated to Ramakrishna Ashram, Belgaum, for youth development programme.

Bangalore
January 2004

Sudha Murty

How I Taught my Grandmother to Read

When I was a girl of about twelve, I used to stay in a village in north Karnataka with my grandparents. Those days, the transport system was not very good, so we used to get the morning paper only in the afternoon. The weekly magazine used to come one day late. All of us would wait eagerly for the bus, which used to come with the papers, weekly magazines and the post.

At that time, Triveni was a very popular writer in the Kannada language. She was a wonderful writer. Her style was easy to read and very convincing. Her stories usually dealt with complex psychological problems in the lives of ordinary people and were always very interesting. Unfortunately for Kannada literature, she died very young. Even now, after forty years, people continue to appreciate her novels.

One of her novels, called *Kashi Yatre*, was appearing as a serial in the Kannada weekly *Karmaveera* then. It is the story of an old lady and her ardent desire to go to

Kashi or Varanasi. Most Hindus believe that going to Kashi and worshipping Lord Vishweshvara is the ultimate *punya*. This old lady also believed in this, and her struggle to go there was described in that novel. In the story there was also a young orphan girl who falls in love but there was no money for the wedding. In the end, the old lady gives away all her savings without going to Kashi. She says, 'The happiness of this orphan girl is more important than worshipping Lord Vishweshwara at Kashi.'

My grandmother, Krishtakka, never went to school so she could not read. Every Wednesday the magazine would come and I would read the next episode of this story to her. During that time she would forget all her work and listen with the greatest concentration. Later, she could repeat the entire text by heart. My grandmother too never went to Kashi, and she identified herself with the novel's protagonist. So more than anybody else she was the one most interested in knowing what happened next in the story and used to insist that I read the serial out to her.

After hearing what happened next in *Kashi Yatre*, she would join her friends at the temple courtyard where we children would also gather to play hide and seek. She would discuss the latest episode with her friends. At that time, I never understood why there was so much of debate about the story.

Once I went for a wedding with my cousins to the neighbouring village. In those days, a wedding was a great event. We children enjoyed ourselves thoroughly. We would eat and play endlessly, savouring the freedom because all the elders were busy. I went for a couple of days but ended up staying there for a week.

When I came back to my village, I saw my grandmother in tears. I was surprised, for I had never seen her cry even in the most difficult situations. What had happened? I was worried.

'Avva, is everything all right? Are you ok?'

I used to call her Avva, which means mother in the Kannada spoken in north Karnataka.

She nodded but did not reply. I did not understand and forgot about it. In the night, after dinner, we were sleeping in the open terrace of the house. It was a summer night and there was a full moon. Avva came and sat next to me. Her affectionate hands touched my forehead. I realized she wanted to speak. I asked her, 'What is the matter?'

'When I was a young girl I lost my mother. There was nobody to look after and guide me. My father was a busy man and got married again. In those days people never considered education essential for girls, so I never went to school. I got married very young and had children. I became very busy. Later I had grandchildren and always felt so much happiness in cooking and feeding all of you. At times I used to regret not going to school, so I made sure that my children and grandchildren studied well ...'

I could not understand why my sixty-two-year-old grandmother was telling me, a twelve-year-old, the story of her life in the middle of the night. But I knew I loved her immensely and there had to be some reason why she was talking to me. I looked at her face. It was unhappy and her eyes were filled with tears. She was a good-looking lady who was usually always smiling. Even today I cannot forget the worried expression on her face. I leaned forward and held her hand.

'Avva, don't cry. What is the matter? Can I help you in any way?'

'Yes, I need your help. You know when you were away, *Karmaveera* came as usual. I opened the magazine. I saw the picture that accompanies the story of *Kashi Yatre* and I could not understand anything that was written. Many times I rubbed my hands over the pages wishing they could understand what was written. But I knew it was not possible. If only I was educated enough. I waited eagerly for you to return. I felt you would come early and read for me. I even thought of going to the village and asking you to read for me. I could have asked somebody in this village but I was too embarrassed to do so. I felt so very dependent and helpless. We are well-off, but what use is money when I cannot be independent?'

I did not know what to answer. Avva continued.

'I have decided I want to learn the Kannada alphabet from tomorrow onwards. I will work very hard. I will keep Saraswati Pooja day during Dassara as the deadline. That day I should be able to read a novel on my own. I want to be independent.'

I saw the determination on her face. Yet I laughed at her.

'Avva, at this age of sixty-two you want to learn alphabet? All your hair is grey, your hands are wrinkled, you wear spectacles and you work so much in the kitchen...'

Childishly I made fun of the old lady. But she just smiled.

'For a good cause if you are determined, you can overcome any obstacle. I will work harder than anybody but I will do it. For learning there is no age bar.'

The next day onwards I started my tuition. Avva was a wonderful student. The amount of homework she did was amazing. She would read, repeat, write and recite. I was her only teacher and she was my first student. Little did I know then that one day I would become a teacher in Computer Science and teach hundreds of students.

The Dassara festival came as usual. Secretly I bought *Kashi Yatre* which had been published as a novel by that time. My grandmother called me to the puja place and made me sit down on a stool. She gave me a gift of a frock material. Then she did something unusual. She bent down and touched my feet. I was surprised and taken aback. Elders never touch the feet of youngsters. We have always touched the feet of God, elders and teachers. We consider that as a mark of respect. It is a great tradition but today the reverse had happened. It was not correct.

She said, 'I am touching the feet of a teacher, not my grand daughter; a teacher who taught me so well, with so much of affection that I can read any novel confidently in such a short period. Now I am independent. It is my duty to respect a teacher. Is it not written in our scriptures that a teacher should be respected, irrespective of the gender and age?'

I did return namaskara to her by touching her feet and gave my gift to my first student. She opened it and read immediately the title *Kashi Yatre* by Triveni and the publisher's name.

I knew then that my student had passed with flying colours.

BOOKS FOR 'AT LEAST ONE LIBRARY'

I come from a middle-class teacher's family. In my family, as with many other families of teachers, books and knowledge were considered to be more important than money.

In our village, I still remember the way people respected my grandfather. He was certainly not the richest man. He used to sit in front of our house, on a mat below a shady banyan tree. He always held a book in his hand. In the evening people would come to him for his advice. Even the richest man, when passing by, would greet him respectfully. I asked him once.

'Why should the teacher be respected?'

He smiled and told me a story. 'It seems, some friends of Arjuna, the mighty warrior in Mahabharata, asked him why he gave so much of respect to his teacher Dronacharya. Drona was old, not as rich as Arjuna, and never ruled any kingdom. But Arjuna would always sit at his feet respectfully. When asked why, it seems Arjuna replied, "In this life everything perishes over a period of time. Whether it be diamond, beauty, gold or even land. Only one thing withstands this destruction. It is knowledge. The more you give the more you get." A teacher gives knowledge to students and I consider him the richest person. That is the reason a teacher is respected; not for his riches but because he is the source of knowledge.'

As a child, the first expedition I ever made outside my home was to the village library building with my grandfather. The library was situated in a small two-storied structure. There was a shop on the ground floor and on the first floor was the library. A big banyan tree stood next to the building. There was a cement platform under it. In Kannada we call it *katte*. In the evening, all the elders of the village would sit here. My grandfather was one of them. I would accompany him and he would go and sit on the platform after dropping me at the first floor.

It was the first of the many libraries I was to enter. There were cupboards with glass panes so that one could read the titles of the books easily. Newspapers and weeklies were piled up neatly. Tables and chairs were laid for people to sit and read. There was absolute silence. I started reading children's books there and used to be absorbed in them until my grandfather would call me to go home.

Years passed and I became a girl of twelve years. By that time, I had finished reading almost all the books in that little village library. At times I used to feel bored going to the library as there were not many new books.

But still I accompanied my old grandfather to the banyan tree.

One such evening, we were coming back after our outing. I was feeling particularly bored with the library that day. It was dark and the streetlights were blinking. My grandfather could not see too well so I was leading him by his hand.

Suddenly he asked me, 'I will recite half a poem, will you complete it? This is a well-known poem.'

I said I would try. We often played this game and I had learnt many poems like this. He said, 'If I have wings . . .'

I immediately answered without blinking my eyes, 'I will go to the neighbouring village library and read many more books.'

My grandfather stopped in surprise. He said, 'Will you repeat it?'

I repeated, 'I will go to the neighbouring village library and read many more books.'

He laughed and said, 'What an unusual way to complete the poem! Do you know what the original poem is?'

'Yes, I know.
'If I have wings
I will fly in the vast blue sky
I will see beautiful places
I will meet great people
I will search for hidden treasures.'

My grandfather kept quiet. When we reached home he sat down on a mat and called me. He was tired but looked very happy. He took my little hand into his and said, 'Do you know, there was a great man called Andrew Carnegie in USA. He was a billionaire who lived a century back. He willed all his wealth not to his children, but to build library buildings in as many villages as possible. I have not seen America, but it seems any library you see in any village was invariably built using Andrew Carnegie's money.

'I do not know how long I will live, but today I realized how much you love books from the way you completed the poem. Promise me, when you grow up, if you have more money than you need, you will buy books for at least one library.'

It was a cold winter night. I still remember the warmth of his large hand in mine. He was old, and his hands had become hard and wrinkled writing thousands of lines on the blackboard with chalk every day. We were not rich like Carnegie, but certainly my grandfather had the richness of experience and knowledge.

Later in my life, I became well off. I remembered my promise of buying books for a library. Today, through Infosys Foundation, we have given books to ten thousand such libraries.

SALAAM ABDUL KALAM

I have been writing columns for a number of newspapers and magazines for a while now. One of them was *The Week* magazine. Writing columns is not an easy job. One has to keep coming up with interesting anecdotes to write about. Sometimes the incident is so nice you feel like writing more but you have to be careful about the word limit. Sometimes you don't get any ideas at all, though the deadline may be nearing. Only very few gifted people can write regular columns for a long time.

Once I wrote a column for *The Week* on the role of Information Technology in people's lives. It was called 'IT Divide'. It was based on a true incident that once happened to me.

Soon after the column appeared, one morning I got a call from Delhi. The operator said, 'Shri Abdul Kalam wants to talk to you.'

That time Abdul Kalam was principal scientific secretary to the Government of India. I had never met him in person till then. I had only read about him in the papers and seen him on TV. Of course I started wondering why a person of his stature would want to talk to an ordinary person like me. We had nothing in common. It would be like a meeting between a Himalayan peak and the peak of Unkal Hill, which is in the small town of Hubli in north Karnataka.

When Abdul Kalam came on the line I said, 'Sir, there is a mistake by the operator. Perhaps you want to speak to my husband, Narayana Murthy?' I knew Murthy knew Mr. Kalam. From the other end a soft, affectionate voice replied, '*Vanakkam*, there is absolutely no mistake. I told the operator to connect to you only.'

I was thrilled.

'Sir, you don't know me but I know a lot about you. I have read about your life in the book *Wings of Fire*.'

'But I too know about you by reading your columns. I read *Ananda Vikatan* regularly where you talk about your dreams and your struggles. Today when I read 'IT Divide' in *The Week*, I laughed and laughed. You have written on a tough topic in such a humorous way! I called my colleagues in the office and told them to read the column. Normally whenever your columns appear, I read the last paragraph first because it contains the gist. Then I read the remaining portion as and when I get time.'

That was the best compliment I had ever received. When I write, I always think of the end first and then the beginning. Kalam seemed to have guessed that in no time.

I had heard from many people that he is extremely simple, wears only white and blue shirts and slippers. Soon

I got to know that this was not an exaggeration. After our talk on the phone I met him several times. Till today, the more I meet him, the more I am convinced about the essential simplicity of the man. Any interaction with him is a joy and I always look forward to that.

I met him for the first time in Bangalore. He sent me word that he wanted to see me though he had a packed schedule. I was waiting for him in a room when he came in, looking cool inspite of a long tough day. For a while we talked about literature and human qualities. He asked me in chaste Tamil, 'How come you know such good Tamil?'

'No sir,' I replied, 'I can't speak Tamil whereas I can understand. My translator, Mr. Arokia Velu is an excellent translator. The credit for what appears in *Ananda Vikatan* should go to him.'

As we chatted, a man without a prior appointment wanted to enter. Kalam's security personnel were reluctant to let him enter. Finally Mr. Kalam said, 'Please allow him. It does not matter. He might have come from a long distance.'

A middle-aged man entered the room along with a photographer. He was holding a huge album and a bag. He told Kalam, 'Sir, I own this institution,' and kept the album in front of him. 'Please come for our prize distribution day. It will be a great honour for all of us.'

Kalam looked at a few pages of the album and said, 'I am short of time so I will not be able to make it. May God bless the children.'

Then the man requested for a photograph with Kalam,

to which he agreed immediately. The gentleman took a pink-coloured shawl from his bag and told the photographer to take his photo while he was laying the shawl on Kalam's shoulder.

The photograph was duly taken and Kalam thanked him and continued talking to me. But my attention was still on the man. I noticed that he took back the shawl and walked out of the room. I could not control my anger.

'Sir, he has taken the shawl which he presented to you.'

Kalam smiled at me and said, 'It does not matter. I don't need any one of them. Probably he needs it.'

Each time I meet him, I am amazed at his straightforward behaviour and his secular outlook. He has a compassionate heart which particularly loves all children.

After that meeting, whenever I was in Chennai, I would see him in his chamber in Anna University where he was teaching. We would talk about many issues, the main one being about education, particularly in the rural areas. He is extremely grateful to his teachers and holds them in the highest respect.

Once I was sharing my experiences in Chandipur, Orissa and a lesson I learnt from a young fisherboy called Javed. He was a poor schoolboy who helped his mother sell red crabs. For an entire day's work he received only Rs 5. Yet he was happy and enthusiastic. When I asked him how he could always remain so optimistic, he said, 'It is better to be worn out than to be rusted.'

As soon as I told this story to him, Kalam wrote Javed's words down on a piece of paper and exclaimed what a great piece of advice it was. He told me that he likes Orissa immensely, as he had spent many years in that state doing missile tests.

'If you are doing something in Orissa I will definitely come. I know you work there and that state is very dear to your heart too.'

Once, I decided to visit Rameshwaram, along with a group of friends. When Kalam got to know, he was very eager to go with us as it is his birth place. He said he would join us in Madurai railway station. He had made all the arrangements when his nomination for the post of President of India was announced. He told me, 'We will keep the plan open for Rameshwaram.'

By this time I was sure he was going to be the President of India irrespective of the election. We could not ask him to join us as it could be major security problem for him. Sadly I had to tell him, 'No sir, please do not come. We will go on our own.'

By the time we returned from the trip, he had, as I had predicted, been elected the President. He invited me to his swearing-in ceremony in the central hall of Parliament. What I saw when I stepped into the hall amazed me. It was filled with children, teachers, his family members, odd people like me and Father George, who used to be my student in Bangalore and then was doing his research under Kalam in Anna University.

It was a most unusual oath-taking ceremony. Everyone seemed to be close to Kalam. Normally such ceremonies are attended by industrialists, politicians and other VIPs. But here there were students, teachers, scientists, ordinary middle-class people and friends of Kalam. I saw Mrinalini Sarabhai, whose husband the late Dr Vikram Sarabhai was also a great scientist and knew Kalam well. Her sister, Captain Laxmi had contested against Kalam for the post of President. She too was present in the audience.

I came away from the function feeling deeply moved by the love I saw everyone showering on Kalam. After a few months, I asked my son, who is a teenager, to meet Kalam.

My son said, 'Amma, he is the President of our country. He is a learned and well respected scientist. He is a very busy man. What will he talk about to a person like me?'

'Child, please understand. I knew him before he became the President and I have met him after he became President. There is absolutely no change. He loves talking to people of your age. That is his mission. He interacts with children through email and chat. That is the reason I want you to meet him. Learn from him those qualities which you will never learn in any university.'

Somehow my son was not very convinced. 'He is too big a man for me,' he muttered.

Nevertheless, he was there when we had dinner with Kalam. For the next two hours they hijacked the entire conversation. Murthy and I could only sit and listen. They discussed the best operating systems for computers, the great Tamil saint Thiruvalvar and his teachings, the future of the children of India, teaching methodologies in America, etc. After he left, my son told me, 'Amma, I never felt that I was talking to the President of India. Rather, it was like talking to my grandfather whom I loved so much and lost four years back. Amma, what you said was true and not at all an exaggeration.'

When Kalam went by train on a tour of Bihar, he invited me to go with him along with five other friends. There I saw another face of Kalam. He would work more than all of us. His schedule would start at 6.30 or 7 a.m. and end at 10.30 or 11 p.m. At seventy-one years he was tireless and the most enthusiastic person in the team all of whom were much younger to him.

He would regularly address large groups of students followed by question-answer sessions. He would take individual questions and answer them. Then he would make children recite some of the important lines after him. He reminded me of a loving schoolteacher or a doting grandfather or an excellent friend to these children irrespective of the difference in age.

During Bangalore's IT.Com I watched him taking an internet class for thousand students. He held their complete attention and was excellently prepared.

When we built a 150-bed Paediatric Hospital in Bhubaneshwar, Orissa for poor children, I was very keen that he should come and inaugurate it. I remembered his promise made to me in Chennai that he would come to Orissa if I invited him. But now he was the President of India, and there were many people like me inviting him to similar functions. He was no longer a professor at Anna University whom I could approach on telephone or send an email and convey my message. However, remembering his promise, I sent him an email assuming it may not reach. But within a few days, I got a reply from his secretary saying that he had agreed to inaugurate the hospital. Coincidentally, it was the eve of Buddha Poornima, May 15, 2003. I have heard many stories about Buddha who was born 2,500 years ago. I was fortunate that this great teacher and lover of children could at least inaugurate and appreciate our effort.

HASSAN'S ATTENDANCE PROBLEM

For many years now, I have been teaching computer science to students studying for their Master's in Computer Applications at a college in Bangalore. I have interacted with many students, and though it is not possible to remember all of them now, the memories of some are etched in my mind. That is not because they were all brilliant, but rather because something in them was very different from the others.

In my first batch, there was a very bright boy called Hassan. He was tall, handsome, with a very good memory. He came from an affluent family where he was the only son. Initially I did not come to know of his existence at all, mainly because he was hardly ever present. I normally take the first class of the day, which is scheduled at 9 a.m., or the one after that at 10 a.m. I prefer this time as this is when students are fresh and very attentive.

Once in a while Hassan would turn up, particularly if

there was a class test or during examinations. I met him more often for attendance shortage meetings. He would beg for attendance in such a manner that it was very difficult for me to say 'no'. Sometimes I would get upset and tell him, 'No, I can't give you attendance. There should be discipline.'

'Yes Madam,' he would reply apologetically, 'pardon me. From the next semester onwards I will definitely attend your class. Can you not pardon me this time? To err is human, to forgive is divine. You have only taught us this.'

I could not remain angry for long. Teachers do get upset with students who are not regular, but if the attendance shortage affects their appearance in the final examination, then one tends to melt like snow against the sun. A good teacher will always wish for the best for her student, though I do agree discipline is very important too.

As he was very bright, Hassan would invariably get a first class in the exam. However, before the exams started, every semester this drama with Hassan would be repeated. I would get upset, threaten and ultimately give in. Each time Hassan would promise to improve his attendance record, and for one week would attend all classes, then the same old story would follow. Each time he had a different reason for his absences. Unfortunately, they always seemed genuine to me.

Once I got tired of his stories and called his parents.

'Your son is a bright boy, he is not arrogant but he is indisciplined. If only he came to class regularly and attended the lab I am sure he can get a rank. I have failed to convince him. I will be happy if you could look into the matter more seriously, because this is going to affect his life,' I said to them.

Hassan's father was a busy man and did not take my words very seriously. He said, 'As long as he does well that is fine with me because after a certain age children do not listen to their parents. Only life will teach them.'

But his mother was in tears.

'Madam, I have failed as a mother. He does not listen to me at all. He spends all night listening to music, and chatting with his friends. He sleeps at six in the morning. How can he come to any class? He does not pay any attention to what I say and tells me I repeat the same thing always.'

The meeting ended in an argument between his parents. His father said, 'You are the mother. It is your duty to correct him. You spend more time with him. I am so busy. You have failed.'

His mother said, 'You are the father. It is difficult to control boys. You can speak to him man to man. Earning money is not the only thing in life.'

This continued for a while and the meeting ended fruitlessly. Hassan continued in his ways till he passed out of his course, as usual in first class. He was a nice boy. He came and thanked me.

'Madam, thank you for teaching me for the last three years. Because of your kind heart I could get all my attendance. I wish all teachers were like you in the college.'

I laughed.

'God willing, we will meet again.'

But I did not meet Hassan for a long time and forgot all about him. Years passed. I taught many students. Some of them became very good human beings, some became famous, some became rich and some remained ordinary. As far as I was concerned, they were like my children. Some remember me still and send invitations to weddings, naming ceremonies, house warmings, etc. If I am in town I definitely try and attend, because for me their immense love is my strength.

One Monday morning, my secretary told me a person wanting to sell the latest software in high school teaching wanted to meet me. I was extremely busy and the piles of unanswered letters were looking at me accusingly. I had no time to talk to a sales person. So I told her, 'He can meet someone else. I don't have time.'

But my secretary said he was insisting he wanted to meet only me and that he was my student. She knew how fond I was of all my students, so she had been unable to say 'no' to him.

'In that case let him see me at 2 p.m.'

In the afternoon, a man of about thirty-five years, plump, with a bald head and moderately dressed was waiting for me in the office. In his hand was the CD with the software. I could not place him though he seemed familiar. He smiled at me and said, 'Madam, can you recognize me? You may not, because how can you remember all your students? From a window you can see the outside world but from the outside you cannot see all that is inside.'

I liked his analogy and was sure he was my student because I often used this phrase in my class. Still I could not guess who he was.

'Madam, I was the perpetual latecomer of your class.'

That's when the coin dropped. 'Hi Hassan. How are you? It's been a long time since I last met you.' I was very happy to see him.

'Madam, I am fine and remember many of your lessons.'

'Is it Database Management? Or C? Or Pascal?'

'None of the software Madam, I remember the moral lessons.'

I didn't know what moral lessons I had taught, though I do tell some stories during my lectures on computer software.

'Hassan, what are you doing now?'

Now his face became a little pale.

'Madam, I am selling this software which is useful in teaching Maths, Physics and Chemistry. It is of help to both teachers and students. I know your foundation helps a lot in education at the high school level. I thought it may be of some interest to you.'

'Hassan, what did you do for so many years?'

I knew all his classmates by this time were in very high positions in the software industry. Hassan being a bright student, should have definitely done well. Yet, on the contrary, he seemed to be doing a small job of selling high school software door-to-door.

'Madam, you know I was very irregular in college. The same habit continued even after my graduation. I would get up late and was very lazy. My mother would lose her temper and peace of mind. I did not bother. I took her for granted. After a lot of pressure from my parents I took up a job. But I continued with the same habits of going late to office, not keeping appointments and not being responsible. I did not have the proper knowledge also. In college, I hardly studied. Getting a first class in the examination is not an index of the amount of knowledge one has. I would study just before the exams, guess the probable questions, and skip the chapters. I always thought I could somehow make it later. But without proper knowledge it is difficult to work. I always laughed at those people who were hard workers. I used to make fun of them and called them "nerds". Today those "nerds" have become millionaires. Nobody liked me in my office because of my behaviour. No employer would keep such an employee, and I lost whatever job I took up. In my frustration I started quarrelling at office as well as at home. Finally my father got so fed up he told me to stay separately. He always gave me a lot of freedom but I never picked up any good habits. My state today is the result of my own habits.'

I felt sorry for Hassan, who with all his intelligence and good nature, could not make it.

'Hassan, you knew your faults, you could have improved and made a better life for yourself. There is always a start at any age. Don't get disappointed. You may have lost a battle but you can still win the war.'

'Madam, old habits die hard.'

'But Hassan it is possible to change your habits. There

is nothing which is impossible. You only require will power. You are yourself not aware of all your potential. Please remember when elders say some thing they do so because they want you to lead a better life than them. Excellence does not come by accident but by practice.'

I could see a twinkle in his eyes. I thought I saw a glimpse of the young bright Hassan. 'I will try my best, Madam,' he promised, as he rose to leave.

I have not met Hassan since that day. I hope to bump into him unexpectedly once again, and this time find him happy and successful.

THE RED RICE GRANARY

Every year, our country has to face natural disasters in some form. It may be an earthquake in Gujarat, floods in Orissa or a drought in Karnataka. In a poor country, these calamities create havoc.

In the course of my work, I have found that after such calamities, many people like to donate money or materials to relief funds. We assume that most donations come from rich people, but that is not true. On the contrary, people from the middle class and lower middle class, help more. Rarely do rich people participate wholeheartedly.

A few years back, I was invited to a reputed company in Bangalore to deliver a lecture on Corporate Social Responsibility. Giving a speech is easy. But I was not sure how many people in the audience would really understand the speech and change themselves.

After my talk was over, I met many young girls and boys. It was an affluent company and the employees were well-off and well-dressed. They were all very emotional after the lecture.

'Madam, we buy so many clothes every month. Can we donate our old clothes to those people who are affected by the earthquake? Can you co-ordinate and send them?'

Some of them offered other things.

'We have grown-up children, we would like to give their old toys and some vessels.'

I was very pleased at the reaction. It reminded me of the incident in Ramayana where during the construction of the bridge between India and Lanka, every squirrel helped Sri Rama by bringing a handful of sand.

'Please send your bags to my office. I will see that they reach the right persons.'

Within a week, my office was flooded with hundreds of bags. I was proud that my lecture had proven so effective.

One Sunday, along with my assistants, I opened the bags. What we saw left us amazed and shocked. The bags were brimming over with all kinds of junk! Piles of high-heeled slippers (some of them without the pair), torn undergarments, unwashed shirts, transparent, cheap saris, toys which had neither shape nor colour, unusable bedsheets, aluminium vessels, broken cassettes were soon piled in front of us like a mountain. There were only a few good shirts, saris and usable materials.

It was apparent that instead of sending the material to a garbage or the kabariwala, these people had transferred them to my office in the name of donation. The men and women I had met that day were bright, well travelled, well-off people. If educated people like them behaved like this, what would uneducated people do?

But then I was reminded of an incident from my childhood. I was born and brought up in a village in Karnataka's Haveri District, called Shiggaon. My grandfather was a retired schoolteacher and my grandmother Krishtakka never went to school. Both of them hardly travelled and had never stepped out of Karnataka. Yet they were hardworking people, who did their work wholeheartedly without expecting anything from anybody in their life. Their photographs never appeared in any paper, nor did they go up on a stage to receive a prize for the work they did. They lived like flowers with fragrance in the forest, enchanting everyone around them, but hardly noticed by the outside world.

In the village we had paddy fields and we used to store the paddy in granaries. There were two granaries. One was in the front and the other at the back of our house. The better quality rice which was white, was always stored in the front granary and the inferior quality, which was a little thick and red, was stored in the granary at the back.

In those days, there was no communal divide in the village. People from different communities lived together in peace. Many would come to our house to ask for alms. There were Muslim fakirs, Hindu Dasaiahs who roamed the countryside singing devotional songs, Yellamma Jogathis who appeared holding the image of Goddess Yellamma over their heads, poor students and invalid people.

We never had too much cash in the house and the only help my grandfather could give these people was in the form of rice. People who receive help do not talk too much. They would receive the rice, smile and raise their right hand to bless us. Irrespective of their religion, the blessing was always 'May God bless you.' My grandfather always looked happy after giving them alms.

I was a little girl then and not too tall. Since the entrance to the front granary was low, it was difficult for grown-ups to enter. So I would be given a small bucket and sent inside. There I used to fill up the bucket with rice and give it to them. They would tell me how many measures they wanted.

In the evening, my grandmother used to cook for everybody. That time she would send me to the granary at the back of the house where the red rice was stored. I would again fill up the bucket with as much rice as she wanted and get it for her to cook our dinner.

This went on for many years. When I was a little older, I asked my grandparents a question that had been bothering me for long.

'Why should we eat the red rice always at night when it is not so good, and give those poor people the better quality rice?'

My grandmother Krishtakka smiled and told me something I will never forget in my life.

'Child, whenever you want to give something to somebody, give the best in you, never the second best. That is what I have learned from life. God is not there in the temple, mosque or church. He is with the people. If you serve them with whatever you have, you have served God.'

My grandfather answered my question in a different way.

'Our ancestors have taught us in the Vedas that one should,

Donate with kind words.

Donate with happiness.

Donate with sincerity.

Donate only to the needy.

Donate without expectation because it is not a gift. It is a duty.

Donate with your wife's consent.

Donate to other people without making your dependents helpless.

Donate without caring for caste, creed and religion.

Donate so that the receiver prospers.'

This lesson from my grandparents, told to me when I was just a little girl, has stayed with me ever since. If at all I am helping anyone today, it is because of the teachings by those simple souls. I did not learn them in any school or college.

THE REAL JEWELS

The district of South Canara in Karnataka is very different from any other. The literacy rate here is high, people are enterprising and hard working. They have travelled all over the world in search of employment. If you see any Udupi vegetarian restaurant in India or any part of the globe, it is sure to have been started by a person from South Canara.

The Infosys Foundation has a project called 'A Library for Every School'. In this we donate books mainly to government school libraries, so that children have easy access to a variey of books. For this, I travel extensively in rural areas and donate books written in Kannada on various subjects. All the travelling has helped me to understand what children want to read in different places. During my travels, I frequently stay in the houses of people I meet, as often there are no hotels in the small towns and villages I visit. Most of the time I stay with the family of a teacher from the school I am visiting. Some times I stay with people I had never met earlier.

In India, a guest is always treated with a lot of love, affection and respect. An old Sanskrit saying is '*Atithi Devo Bhava*', meaning God comes in the form of a guest.

I have felt this to be so true, especially during my stay in villages. The poorest of the poor have treated me with so much love and affection. They have given me the best hospitality possible without knowing who I am or expecting anything in return.

In 1998, I went to a village in South Canara for a school function. It was the rainy season and the small village was on the coast of the Arabian Sea. It was pouring and there were no hotels in the village. The school teacher was a bachelor and lived in a rented room. He told me, 'Madam, the chairman of this school is a fine gentleman. He has asked me to tell you that you could stay tonight with his family. You cannot travel today because of this rain. Even the bridge has gone under water.'

I did not have much option. I felt a little uncomfortable staying with someone I had never even met. By that time the chairman Mr. Aithappa came with an umbrella to call me. He had been caught up in some important work and not been able to attend the function.

His house was huge. It was functional without much decoration. There was a big granary room and a storage place for coconuts and vegetables. It had red oxide flooring and was like many traditional houses of South Canara where there was an inside courtyard. Water had to be drawn from a well at the side of the kitchen. There were a few bedrooms on the ground floor and the first floor. There was a cowshed at the back, along with a large vegetable garden. That was all I could see as it was already dark and the raindrops were hitting me like pebbles hard on my feet.

As soon as I entered, the lady of the house came with a warm smile and towels to wipe myself. Her smile put me instantly at ease. Without much ceremony she said, 'Please feel comfortable. Dinner will be ready in half an hour.'

I changed my dress and came to the dining hall. In the huge hall there were only four people including me, the couple and their elderly mother. Plantain leaves were laid on the floor and the cook was serving. There were innumerable food items and I did not know where to start. The old lady of the house was very gracious. She reminded me of my large-hearted grandmother. After dinner I wanted to chat with her. When I told her, she said, 'If you want you can stay in my room so that we can talk.' I preferred that, rather than staying all alone in the first-floor guest room.

I have always wondered why people in South Canara are so much more educated, compared to any other district of Karnataka. I asked Kuttamma, 'Did you study when you were young?'

Kuttamma sighed as if she was in pain.

'No, unfortunately I did not go to school. When I was young we were extremely poor and I was a coolie in the garden of a school teacher. I always felt education is essential. If you can read and write you can secure a better job. In my case it was not possible. So I was determined that my only son Aithappa should study as much as he could and I would work hard for that. My husband also felt the same way, but he was killed by a snake-bite when my son was only five years old. It was my promise to him that I would educate my son.'

I tried to imagine life six decades back—the social pressures, the great poverty, and no help from the government. I have met many women of that age group who have told me more or less the same story. Kuttamma continued.

'My son did not disappoint me. He went to Bombay as a hotel boy. He cleaned the plates in the morning, and in the evenings went to Moghaveera night school and studied there.'

'Yes, I know this school. It is in Worli and is the oldest Kannada school in Bombay. Many children have studied there.'

'Once he finished his schooling he became a clerk at the counter of a hotel and went to night college. He got his degree and started his own hotel in Bombay. He became very successful.'

'Then why is he here now?'

Kuttamma smiled. I could see she was proud.

'He started many hotels in Bombay but I remained in my village. I never felt comfortable in Bombay inspite of all the money he had because nobody spoke my language there and I love this village.'

'Yes, I know there is a saying in Sanskrit:
Janani Janmabhoomischa
Swargadapi gariyasi
It means your motherland is always a heaven.'

'You are a learned lady so you can recite all this in Sanskrit but my intuition told me to stay here and do something for our own people. My son became very wealthy and handed over his business to his son. He is now sixty-five years old and ten years back he returned to his village.'

'How does he spend his time?'

I could understand the old lady not wanting to move out of her home but I was unable to understand how a busy successful person like Aithappa could retire to this godforsaken sleepy village.

'When he became rich, my son asked me, "Amma, I have earned so much wealth. I want to know what you want. I remember you sold all your jewellery for my fees in college, you had only one meal so that I could have two. Now I want to buy lots of jewellery for you."'

'What did you answer?'

'I told my son that in life, the real jewellery is education. The school teacher for whom I worked when I was young used to tell everything will perish over a period of time—flowers, beauty, food. No person looks beautiful forever. But education brings confidence to your face and that is the real beauty. I have crossed the age to wear jewelleries. If you respect my wishes, build as many free schools as possible in as many villages in South Canara. My son understood my feelings. He himself shifted to this village and has, till today, built ten such schools. He remains very busy managing these schools.'

Now I understood the reason behind the high literacy rate of the area. Women like Kuttamma had not studied but they had understood the importance of good education. They had insisted their children go to school. It is certainly true that if one man studies, only one person is educated whereas if one lady studies, the entire family is educated.

A History Lesson on Teachers' Day

The date was September 5th 2003, or Teachers' Day. In Bangalore, on that day, I have a great time with my students. If, for some reason, I am out of Bangalore, I miss all the celebrations. On Teachers' Day, my students take me out and we all have lunch together and also watch a movie. They pool in their money and refuse to let me pay for anything. It shows me how close they are to me and that they remember me. It is an act of love and affection for their teacher. Each of them will go their different ways after they complete the course, but love, affection and concern for each other will always bind us together.

Last year, on Teachers' day, I was out of station on some work and feeling depressed. A friend of mine realized that and said, 'Let us go watch a film, you will feel better.'

We went to the theatre. There was a big queue. I was surprised because there were only students from schools and colleges in the queue. As my friend was getting the tickets, I remembered my students and started chatting with the youngsters.

'How come you people are here? Is there no celebration in your college or school?'

They were a group of girls. One of them replied.

'Why should there be a celebration in the school?'

'Is it not Teachers' Day?'

'So what? We knew there was a holiday, we did not even ask for what. Today being Saturday, we are very happy that we are getting two days of holidays.'

'Why? Does your school not celebrate Teachers' Day? Do you know why September 5th is known as Teachers' Day?'

Another girl replied. 'Our school may be celebrating Teachers' Day but we don't want to go. We see the same teachers every day. Why see them even on a holiday?'

That provoked the teacher in me. I asked, 'Tell me, what do we celebrate on November 14th, October 2nd, August 15th and January 26th?'

'We know they are holidays but not sure for what.'

One of them shyly said, 'I know October 2nd is Gandhi's birthday.'

At least they knew one answer! 'How come you know only that day?'

'Because it is my birthday. My grandfather was a freedom fighter. He named me Mohini and he told me Gandhiji's name was Mohandas.'

'So Mohini, do you like your name?'

'No, I don't like it. It is very old-fashioned. It sounds like it belongs to someone living a century ago. I have changed my name to Monica.'

Some other girl told me, 'I get confused with August 15th and January 26th. One of them is Independence Day and the other one is something connected with independence.'

I refused to give up. 'Tell me, when did we get independence?'

That started off a discussion in the group. I could make out a number of opinions were being debated. One said 1950, some others said 1942 and the third group said 1947. In fact the 1942-group was very sure they were right as they had watched the movie *1942 A Love Story*.

'Do you know who was India's President then?'

'We know it is Abdul Kalam.'

'No, I am asking you before him.'

They were blank.

'Have you heard of Dr Sarvapalli Radhakrishnan?'

'We know about Radhakrishna. Their statues in marble are very beautiful. I have seen them in the Hare Rama Hare Krishna temple. I went with my parents,' one of them replied.

I told them, 'Dr Sarvapalli Radhakrishnan was a famous philosopher and a great teacher. He taught in Calcutta, Mysore and Banaras. When he left Mysore, it seems students pulled the carriage to the station themselves and not horses. For his lectures, students from other colleges would come and listen, irrespective of the subjects they were studying. He was acknowledged as the best teacher wherever he taught. Later he became the President of India. Hence his birthday was declared as Teachers' Day. There are many stories about him. Please read any book or see on the internet.'

The group looked ashamed now. I felt bad and realized it was not their fault alone. We give holidays to children but do not tell them the reason behind the holiday. Every year we prepare the same boring speech and deliver it to a handful of children. Most of us take the day off and do not make any effort so that children look forward to the day. We could make them plant trees and teach them about the environment; or we could take them out for a picnic and get close to them outside the classroom. It is our duty to make sure that days like Teachers' Day are utilized properly. We have to work hard for that, which we don't do. Children should be led by example and teachers are the best examples. What we preach, we should practise.

'APPRO J.R.D.'

There are two photographs that hang on my office wall. Every day when I enter my office I look at them and start my day. They are pictures of two old people. One is of a gentleman in a blue suit and the other one is a black and white photograph of an old man with dreamy eyes and a white beard.

Many people have asked me if they are related to me. Some people have even asked me, 'Is this black and white photo that of a Sufi saint or a religious guru?'

I smile and reply 'No, nor are they related to me.'

'Then why do you look at them and start the day?'

'These people made an impact on my life. I am grateful to them.'

'Who are these people?'

'The man in the blue suit is Bharat Ratna J.R.D. Tata and the black and white photo is of Sir Jamsetji Tata.'

'But why do you have their photos in your office?'

'You can call it gratitude.'

Then, invariably, I have to tell the person the following story. It happened a long time ago. I was young and bright, bold and idealistic. I was studying in the final year for my Master's degree in Computer Science at Indian Institute of Science, Bangalore, which was then known as the Tata Institute. For me, life was full of fun and joy. I did not know what helplessness or injustice meant.

It was probably the April of 1974. Bangalore was just becoming warm. Red Gulmohars were blooming at the IISc campus. I was the only girl in my post-graduate department in Engineering, and was staying in the ladies' hostel. Other girls were pursuing their research in different departments of science.

After completing my post-graduation, I was keen to go abroad to do my doctorate in Computer Science and had already been offered scholarships from universities in USA. I had not thought of taking up a job in India.

One day, while on the way to my hostel from the lecture hall, I saw an advertisement on the notice board.

It was a standard job requirement notice from the famous automobile company TELCO. It stated that the company required young, bright engineers, hard working with excellent academic background, etc.

At the bottom there was a small line: 'Lady candidates need not apply'.

I read it and was very upset. For the first time, I was faced with gender discrimination.

Though I was not keen on taking up a job, I took it as a challenge and decided to apply. I had done extremely

well in my studies, probably better than most of the boys.
Little did I know then that in real life, to be successful,
academic excellence is not a necessary condition.

After reading the notice, I went fuming to my room.
There I decided not only to apply for the job, but also to
inform the top-most person of the management of TELCO
about the injustice. I got a postcard and started to write.
But there was a problem. Who was the head of TELCO?
I did not know. I was so ignorant that I thought it must be
one of the Tatas. I knew JRD Tata was the head of the
Tata Group. I had seen his pictures in newspapers.
Actually, Sumant Mulgoankar was then its Chairman,
which I was not aware.

I took the postcard and started writing. Even now I
clearly remember what I had written to JRD.

'Tatas have always been pioneers. They are the people
who started the basic infrastructure industries in India
like iron and steel, chemicals, textiles, locomotives, etc.
They have cared for higher education in India since 1900,
and are responsible for the establishment of the Indian
Institute of Science! Fortunately I study there. But I am
surprised that in such a company you can make a
distinction between men and women?'

I posted the letter that was written in anger, and after
a few days forgot about it.

Within ten days, I received a telegram stating that I
had to appear for an interview at TELCO Pune, at their
expense. I was taken aback. But my hostel-mates told me
I had to use the opportunity to go to Pune free of cost.
And the reason? Pune saris were cheap! I was told to buy

saris for them. I even collected thirty rupees per head for each of their saris. Now, when I look back, I feel like laughing at the reasons but then they seemed good ones to make a trip.

This was my first visit to Pune. I fell in love with the city and even to this date it is very dear to my heart. I feel as much at home in Pune as I do at Hubli. The city changed my life in so many ways.

As directed, I went to TELCO's Pimpri office for the interview. There were six people on the panel and it was only then that I realized this was serious business.

'This is the girl who wrote to JRD,' I heard them whisper to each other as soon as I entered. By then I knew for sure that I would not get a job. And when I wouldn't get a job, why should I be scared? So I was rather cool for the interview.

Even before they started the interview I knew they were biased so I told them, rather rudely, 'I hope this is only a technical interview.'

They were taken aback by my rudeness, and even today I am ashamed of my attitude.

During the interview they asked many technical questions and I answered all of them. Then one elderly gentleman with an affectionate voice told me, 'Do you know why we said that lady candidates need not apply? The reason is that to this day we have not employed any ladies on the shop floor of the factory. This is an automobile industry. Trainees may have to work in shifts. For training, we may have to send them to Jamshedpur in Bihar. All our plants have men and machinery. Our trainees may have to drive. We have a trainee's hostel and a guesthouse for them. If a lady enters, then how can we accommodate her? We do not know how men on the shop floor will accept her. How will she come for shifts? We care for our employees, particularly if she is a lady. It is not a college where there is no gender difference. This is a factory. When it comes to academics, you are a first ranker throughout. We appreciate that. People like you should work more in research laboratories.'

I was a young girl from small-town Hubli. My world was very small. I did not know the ways of large corporate houses and their difficulties. So I answered, 'But somewhere you must start. Otherwise a lady will never be able to work in the factories. You are pioneers in many aspects of life. When I look at your industries, you are far ahead of other people. If you think this way, then how will any lady ever enter this so-called man's domain?'

'Training a candidate costs a lot to our company. You are of a marriageable age. After your training you will leave this company and shift to wherever your husband works. Is it not a waste of money for us?'

I thought for a moment and replied, 'I definitely agree with what you say. I am sure when many of you married, your wives came along with you. That has been our tradition. But is it also not true that many men undergo training, and just for a few more hundred rupees, they shift their jobs. You don't have any rule for them. You can't stop them.'

Finally, after a long interview, I was told I had been successful in securing a job at TELCO. On the way back,

I got down at Hubli, my home town. I was eager to meet my father, always my best friend, and tell him my adventure. I was sure he would be happy and praise me.

But I was in for a shock. He was very upset. He said, 'You should have basic manners when addressing elderly people like JRD Tata. You should have written the letter more politely and put it in an envelope, instead of sending a postcard. Now you have to take up this job because you are morally responsible.'

That is what my future had in store for me. Never ever had I thought I would take up a job at Pune. There I met a shy young man from Karnataka, we became good friends and married.

The elderly gentleman who interviewed me was Dr. Sathya Murty, who was an excellent technocrat and human being. I worked with him for some years. After joining TELCO I realized who JRD was. He was the uncrowned king of Indian industry. I did not get to meet him until I was transferred to Bombay. JRD had an office at Bombay House, the headquarters of Tata Industries.

One day, I was supposed to show some reports to our Chairman Mr. Mulgoankar, whom everyone always referred to as SM. So I went to his office on the first floor of Bombay House.

While I was in SM's room, JRD walked in. That was the first time I saw 'Appro JRD'. 'Appro' means 'ours' in Gujarati. In Bombay House people used to affectionately call him 'Appro JRD'.

By this time, I knew who he was and was feeling very nervous, remembering my rude postcard to him.

SM introduced me very nicely, 'Jeh look, this young girl is an engineer and that too a post-graduate. She has worked on the shop-floor at TELCO. Is it not unusual? She was the first girl in our TELCO shop-floor.'

JRD looked at me. I was praying he would not ask me any questions regarding my interview or the postcard. Thankfully he didn't ask me anything about that. Instead he remarked, 'It is nice that in our country girls are getting into engineering. By the way, what is your name?'

'When I joined TELCO I was Sudha Kulkarni, Sir. Now I am Sudha Murty.'

'Where do you work?'

'At Nanavati Mahalaya,' I replied.

He smiled at me nodding his head and the two men started their discussion. I just ran out of the room.

After that I used to see JRD on and off. He was the Chairman of a large group of companies and I was only an engineer in one of those companies. There was nothing we had in common. I used to look at him with awe.

One day I was waiting for Murthy to come and pick me up after office hours. To my surprise, I saw JRD standing next to me. I did not know how to react. I was feeling uneasy. Again I started worrying about the postcard. Now when I look back, I realize JRD must have forgotten about it. It must have been a very small incident to him but not so for me.

He asked me, 'Young lady, why are you here? Office time is over.' I said, 'Sir, I am waiting for my husband to come and pick me up'.

JRD said, 'It is getting dark. There's no one in the

corridor. I will wait with you until your husband comes.'

I was quite used to waiting for Murthy so I was not bothered much by having to wait in the dark. But having JRD waiting along with me made me very uncomfortable. Out of the corner of my eye I looked at him.

He wore a simple white pant and shirt. He was old yet his face was glowing, without any air of superiority.

I was thinking, 'Look at this person. He is the Chairman, a well-respected man in our country and he is waiting for the sake of an ordinary lady employee.'

As soon as I saw Murthy I rushed out.

JRD called and said, 'Young lady, tell your husband never to be late and make his wife wait.'

In 1982 I had to resign from my job at TELCO. I was very reluctant to resign but did not have a choice. Even now, my love and respect for the House of Tatas is the same. I always looked up to JRD as my role model for his simplicity, generosity, kindness and the care he took of his employees.

After I had made my final settlements with the company, I was coming down the steps of Bombay House when I saw JRD coming up. He was absorbed in some thought. I wanted to say goodbye to him. So I stopped. He saw me and he also stopped.

Gently he said, 'So what are you doing Ms. Kulkarni?' (That was the way he always addressed me.)

'Sir I am leaving TELCO.'

'Where are you going?'

'Pune, Sir. My husband is starting a company called Infosys. So I have to shift to Pune.'

'Oh! What will you do when you are successful?'

'Sir I do not know whether we will be successful or not.'

'Never start with diffidence. Always start with confidence. When you are successful, you must give back to society. Society gives us so much, we must return it. I wish you all the best.'

Then JRD continued walking up the stairs. I stood for a while, watching him. That was the last time I saw him alive.

Many years later, I met Ratan Tata in the same Bombay office occupying the same chair as JRD. I told him many of my sweet memories of working with TELCO. I said, 'I cannot call you Mr. Tata like Murthy calls you. You are occupying "Appro JRD's" seat. You will always be "Chairman Sir" to me.'

Later, he wrote to me, 'It was nice listening about Jeh from you. The sad part is that he is not alive today to see you.'

I consider JRD a great man because, inspite of being an extremely busy person, he valued one postcard written by a young girl, who was asking for justice and questioning him. He must have received thousands of letters everyday. He could have thrown mine away in a dustbin. But he didn't do that. He respected the intentions of that unknown girl, who had neither influence nor money and gave her an opportunity to work in his company. He did not merely give her a job, but also changed her life and mindset forever.

Today, in any engineering college I see that forty to

fifty per cent of the students are girls. On the shop floor of many mechanical industries we see so many ladies working. That time I think of JRD fondly.

If at all time stops and asks me what I want from life, I would say I wish JRD were alive today to see how the company we started has grown. He would have enjoyed it wholeheartedly.

HEART OF GOLD

This is a true story. I heard it on the radio during one of my visits to the US. It happened in one of the biggest cities in the world, New York.

It was winter. One evening, a worried mother stood shivering by the road, wearing an old coat. With her was a little girl, thin, sick-looking with a shaven head. She was wearing an oversize dress which somebody had probably given to her out of mercy. It was apparent that they were homeless and poor. The child had a cardboard placard in her hand which said, 'I am suffering from cancer. Please help me.'

The mother was carrying a begging bowl. Whenever the traffic lights turned red they would approach people, stopping them on the road and asking for help.

America is a rich country, but if you are sick and don't have insurance, then you are lost. Nobody can support you. People give small amounts of money when they see such pleas for help. This kind of a scene is not uncommon in India. We see lots of beggars with small infants in one hand and a begging bowl in another. But in America it is not so common. People felt bad for this unfortunate mother and child.

One day, a policeman was passing by and saw them. He asked them a few questions and noticed that the child indeed looked very sick with her swollen eyes and shaven head. He wanted to help, so he opened his purse. He saw a bundle of notes which he had just drawn from the bank. He had received a good bonus for the excellent work he had done. He thought, 'I have a warm home, a caring wife and a loving son. God has been very kind to me. But these unfortunate people don't have any one of these things. It is not their mistake that God has not been kind to them.' He remembered the many things he had promised his wife and son he would buy when he got his bonus. For a while he was in two minds. Then he decided and gave all the cash which he had drawn from the bank to the woman and said, 'Please take good care of the child.'

When he reached home his son met him at the doorstep as usual and hugged him. The house was warm and nice. He sat in front of his wife, and looking at the snow falling outside, he narrated the whole incident. After listening to him for a while his wife was silent, then she smiled. But the son was angry. He said, 'Dad, how are you sure that they have not cheated you? And even though you wanted to give some money you could have given some portion. Why did you give everything?'

The policeman laughed at his son and said, 'Son, you

do not know what poverty is. I come across such unfortunate people in my work.'

The days passed and everybody forgot about it.

One day a news item in the paper caught the son's attention: 'Mother and child caught cheating.' With great interest he read:

'A greedy mother used her healthy child to pose as a cancer patient. She shaved the child's head, starved her and dressed her shabbily so that anybody would feel the child was suffering from cancer. Using this tactic she duped many people. The mother has been arrested.'

The son realized who these people were and was very upset. When his father came home, he told him as soon as he entered the house, 'Dad, you were cheated by that lady and her child who you thought was a cancer patient. The child is healthy and you gave away your entire bonus to that child.'

His father did not reply. He sat down, and looked out of the window. There were children playing outside. Winter was over and summer was setting in. In a calm voice he said, 'Son, I am very happy. The child is healthy.'

The boy was surprised. He thought being a policeman, his father would pick up the phone and talk to the police station or he would be depressed that he had been cheated and given away so much of money to a healthy child. But there were no traces of such emotions.

He asked, 'Dad, tell me, are you not upset?'

His father again gave him the same answer, 'I am happy that the child is healthy.'

By that time his wife came with a mug of coffee in her

hand. She had heard the entire conversation. With happiness in her voice she told her son. 'Son, you are very fortunate. You have an extraordinary father, who is not angry even though he has lost a lot of money. You should be proud that your father is happy thinking somebody's child is healthy, rather than worrying about his own big bonus. Learn from him. Help people without expecting anything in return.'

A WEDDING IN RUSSIA

A wedding is a great event in everyone's life. In India, it is done with a great deal of ceremony. In our films, a large number of stories are based upon weddings.

If you look at Indian history, you will see many wars have been fought for the sake of a marriage. People have always spent a lot of money and effort on these. In olden days the wedding celebrations used to carry on for a week. Later it came down to three days, then two days and now it is for a day. The amount of money spent sometimes constitutes the entire life's savings of a person. At times people take such huge loans for this celebration that they have to go on repaying throughout their lives. In my experience, whenever I have talked to bonded labourers, I have found that a majority of them have got into that state because of the wedding expenses they had incurred.

In a marriage, the couple and their parents are worried about various things. Is she looking pretty? Are the guests being looked after? Will he keep her happy? People like you and me are worried about the wedding lunch. It is an occasion where young boys get to meet young girls, old people talk about their ailments and women exhibit their finest jewellery and silk saris.

Recently I was in Moscow, Russia. Moscow city has many war memorials. Russia has won three great wars in its history, which are a source of pride for them. They have built war memorials and erected many statues of the generals who were responsible for the victories. The first war was between Peter the Great and Sweden. The second was between Tsar Alexander I and Napoleon of France. The third one was against Hitler in World War II in 1945.

There is a huge park in Moscow, known as Peace Park. In the middle of this Peace Park there is a large monument. There is a pillar, and on the pillar the different battles fought by Russia have been mentioned along with dates and places. The park has beautiful fountains. In the summer, flowers of many colours bloom and the place is a feast for the eyes. In the night it is decorated with lights. Every Russian is proud of this park and it is a spot visited by all tourists.

The day I went to the park was Sunday. It was drizzling and cold, though it was summer. I was standing under an umbrella and enjoying the beauty. Suddenly, my eyes fell on a young couple. It was apparent that they had just got married. The girl was in her mid-twenties, slim with blond hair and blue eyes. She was very beautiful. The boy was almost of the same age and very handsome. He was in a military uniform. The bride was wearing a white satin dress, decorated with pearls and pretty laces. It was very long so two young girls were standing behind her holding up the ends of the gown, so it should not be dirtied. One young boy was holding an umbrella over their heads so that they should not get drenched. The girl was holding a bouquet and the two were standing with their arms linked. It was a beautiful sight. I started wondering why they had come to this park in this rain soon after getting married. They could have surely gone to a merrier place. I watched as they walked together to the dais near the memorial, kept the bouquet, bowed their heads in silence and slowly walked back.

By now I was very curious to know what was going on. I could not ask the couple because they probably could not speak English and I didn't know the Russian language. There was an old man standing with them. He looked at me, my sari and asked, 'Are you an Indian?'

I replied, 'Yes, I am an Indian.'

'I have seen Raj Kapoor's movies. They were great. Raj Kapoor had visited Russia. I know one Hindi song *Main awara hoon*'. Do you know Moscow city has statues of three great Indians?'

'Who are they?'

'Jawaharlal Nehru, Mahatma Gandhi and Indira Gandhi.'

Since we were chatting quite amicably now, I decided to use the opportunity to ask some questions.

'How come you know English?'

'Oh, I worked abroad.'

'Will you tell me why that young couple visited the

war memorial on their wedding day?'

'Oh, that is the custom in Russia. The wedding takes place normally on a Saturday or a Sunday. Irrespective of the season, after signing the register at the marriage office, married couples must visit the important national monuments near by. Every boy in this country has to serve in the military for a couple of years at least. Regardless of his position, he must wear his service uniform for the wedding.'

'Why is that?'

'This is a mark of gratitude. Our forefathers have given their lives in the various wars Russia has fought. Some of them we won, and some we lost, but their sacrifice was always for the country. The newly married couple needs to remember they are living in a peaceful, independent Russia because of their ancestors' sacrifices. They must ask for their blessings. Love for country is more important than wedding celebrations. We elders insist on continuing with this tradition whether it be in Moscow, St. Petersburg or any other part of Russia. On the wedding day they have to visit the nearest war memorial.'

This set me wondering about what we teach our children. Do we tell them about the sacrifices of the 1857 War of Independence? Do we talk about the 1942 Quit India movement, or ask newly-weds to visit the Andaman Cellular Jail where thousands lived in solitude and were sent to the gallows? Do we remember Bhagat Singh, Chandrashekhar Azad, Shivaji, Rana Pratap, Lakshmi Bai who gave their lives to save our country?

These men and women never lived to see an

independent India. But do we have the courtesy to remember them on the most important day of our lives? We are busy shopping for saris, buying jewellery and preparing elaborate menus and partying in discos.

My eyes filled with tears at the thought and I wished we could learn a lesson from the Russians.

'AMMA, WHAT IS YOUR DUTY?'

At that time, my daughter Akshata was a teenager. By nature she was very sensitive. On her own, she started reading for blind children at Ramana Maharshi Academy for the Blind at Bangalore. She was a scriber too. She used to come home and tell me about the world of blind people. Later she wrote an essay on them, called 'I Saw the World through the Blind Eyes of Mary'. Mary was a student at the academy who was about to appear for the pre-university exam. Once Akshata took Mary to Lalbagh for a change. The conversation between them was quite unusual.

'Mary, there are different types of red roses in this park,' Akshata told her.

Mary was surprised. 'Akshata, what do you mean by red?'

Akshata did not know how to explain what was red. She took a rose and a jasmine, and gave them to Mary.

'Mary, smell these two flowers in your hand. They have

different smells. The first one is a rose. It is red in colour. The second one is jasmine. It is white. Mary, it is difficult to explain what is red and what is white. But I can tell you that in this world there are many colours, which can be seen and differentiated only through the eyes and not by touch. I am sorry.'

After that incident Akshata told me, 'Amma, never talk about colours when you talk to blind people. They feel frustrated. I felt so helpless when I was trying to explain to Mary. Now I always describe the world to them by describing smells and sounds which they understand easily.'

Akshata also used to help a bright blind boy called Anand Sharma at this school. He was the only child of a schoolteacher from Bihar. He was bright and jolly. He was about to appear for his second pre-university exam.

One day, I was heading for an examination committee meeting. At that time, I was head of the department of Computer Science at a local college. It was almost the end of February. Winter was slowly ending and there was a trace of summer setting in. Bangalore is blessed with beautiful weather. The many trees lining the roads were flowering and the city was swathed in different shades of violet, yellow and red.

I was busy getting ready to attend the meeting, hence I was collecting old syllabi, question papers and reference books. Akshata came upstairs to my room. She looked worried and tired. She was studying in class ten. I thought she was tired preparing for her exams. As a mother I have never insisted they study too much. My parents never did that. They always believed the child has to be responsible. A responsible child will sit down to study on her own.

I told Akshata, 'Don't worry about the exams. Trying is in your hands. The results are not with you.' She was annoyed and irritated by my advice. 'Amma, I didn't talk about any examination. Why are you reminding me of that?'

I was surprised at her irritation. But I was also busy gathering old question papers so did not say anything. Absently, I looked at her face. Was there a trace of sadness on it? Or was it my imagination?

'Amma, you know Anand Sharma. He came to our house once. He is a bright boy. I am confident that he will do very well in his final examination. He is also confident about it. He wants to study further.'

She stopped. By this time I had found the old question papers I had been looking for, but not the syllabus. My search was on. Akshata stood facing me and continued, 'Amma, he wants to study at St. Stephens in Delhi. He does not have anybody. He is poor. It is an expensive place. What should he do? Who will support him? I am worried.'

It was getting late for my meeting so casually I remarked, 'Akshata, why don't you support him?'

'Amma, where do I have the money to support a boy in a Delhi hostel?'

My search was still on.

'You can forfeit your birthday party and save money and sponsor him.'

At home, even now both our children do not get pocket

money. Whenever they want to buy anything they ask me and I give the money. We don't have big birthday parties. Akshata's birthday party would mean calling a few of her friends to the house and ordering food from the nearby fast food joint Shanthi Sagar.

'Amma, when an educated person like you, well-travelled, well-read and without love for money does not help poor people, then don't expect anyone else to do. Is it not your duty to give back to those unfortunate people? What are you looking for in life? Are you looking for glamour or fame? You are the daughter of a doctor, granddaughter of a schoolteacher and come from a distinguished teaching family. If you cannot help poor people then don't expect anyone else to do it.'

Her words made me abandon my search. I turned around and looked at my daughter. I saw a young sensitive girl pleading for the future of a poor blind boy. Or was she someone reminding me of my duty towards society? I had received so much from that society and country but in what way was I returning it? For a minute I was frozen. Then I realized I was holding the syllabus I was looking for in my hand and it was getting late for the meeting.

Akshata went away with anger and sadness in her eyes. I too left for college in a confused state of mind.

When I reached, I saw that as usual the meeting was delayed. Now I was all alone. I settled down in my chair in one of the lofty rooms of the college. There is a difference between loneliness and solitude. Loneliness is boring, whereas in solitude you can inspect and examine your deeds and your thoughts.

I sat and recollected what had happened that afternoon. Akshata's words were still ringing in my mind.

I was forty-five years old. What was my duty at this age? What was I looking for in life?

I did not start out in life with a lot of money. A great deal of hard work had been put in to get where we were today. What had I learnt from the hard journey that was my life? Did I work for money, fame or glamour? No, I did not work for those; they came accidentally to me. Initially I worked for myself, excelling in studies. After that I was devoted to Infosys and my family. Should not the remaining part of my life be used to help those people who were suffering for no fault of theirs? Was that not my duty? Suddenly I remembered JRD's parting advice to me: 'Give back to society.'

I decided that was what I was going to do for the rest of my life. I felt relieved and years younger.

I firmly believe no decision should be taken emotionally. It should be taken with a cool mind and when you are aware of the consequences. After a week I wrote my resignation letter as head of the department and opted only for a teacher's post.

I am ever grateful to Akshata for helping bring this happiness and satisfaction in my work and life. It means more to me than the good ranks I got in school, and my wealth.

When I see hope in the eyes of a destitute, see the warm smile on the faces of once helpless people, I feel so satisfied. They tell me that I am making a difference.

I joined Infosys Foundation as a Founder Trustee. The

Foundation took up a number of philanthropic projects for the benefit of the poor in different states of India.

I received many awards on various occasions. One of them was the *Economic Times* award given to Infosys Foundation. As a trustee I was invited to receive this award. At that time I remembered my guru. Now she was a student in USA. I told her, 'At least for one day you must come for this award ceremony in Bombay. If you had not woken me up at the right time, I would not have been receiving it today. I want you to be present.'

I will remain indebted to Akshata forever for the way she made me change my life and the lesson she taught me.

THE STORY OF TWO DOCTORS

My sister is a doctor in a government hospital. She works very long hours. Often she has to do night duty which can be very exhausting. Our government hospitals may not have too many facilities, but at least the poor can get treatment here for almost free.

Once, during one of her night duties, she had to perform many operations and came home very late. Just as she reached home there was a call from the hospital for her to come and perform another emergency operation. She was about to leave immediately. Seeing her tired face I made a comment. 'I agree patients are very important to doctors. But for the last twenty-four hours you were in the hospital. You are also a human being; you too require rest. You can tell somebody else to do this operation. Why don't you rest now?'

She smiled at me and said, 'It is not me alone. There are many doctors along with me who are working equally hard. They also require rest. I am the senior-most doctor, so I must lead the team. In the larger interest of the people you must sacrifice your personal pain. Don't you remember the story of anaesthesia?' Saying this she went away.

I then remembered the story she had mentioned. My sister had narrated it to me some years ago. To what extent this story is true I don't know. But it is a remarkable one.

Many years ago, in England, there was a father-and-son pair who were doctors. The father was very famous and innovative, and the son was young and enthusiastic. In those days there was no concept of anaesthesia and whenever a patient was to be operated on, chloroform was given.

The senior doctor did many experiments in this field and developed a medicine, which when injected in the area where the operation was to be done, made only that part numb. There was no need to make the patient unconscious. Today we call this local anaesthesia.

He performed several experiments and was convinced by adding different chemicals that his medicine was effective. But there was one problem. No one would offer himself for the experiment. Without experimenting on a human being this medicine could not be officially released in the market.

Now, the doctor's son had six fingers on his left hand. One day, he suggested to his father, 'Father, I know your medicine is very good. You inject it to my sixth finger and operate and remove the finger. Anyway I wanted to get rid of that finger. Let us perform this operation in front of other doctors. No man can stand the pain of surgery without anaesthesia. When they look at my face they will come to know that your medicine has made the area numb and I am not experiencing any pain.'

The suggestion was very good. The father conveyed a message to the members of the Academy of Medical Science, who were the final authority for allowing this medicine to be used in public.

The day of the operation came and several scientists, doctors and other public figures assembled to watch the effect of this miracle injection. The father exhibited his son's sixth finger, and injected the medicine. He said, 'Now I will start the operation. You can observe the patient's face.'

There was a smile on the young man's face. The operation was performed and was a success. Throughout, the smile remained on the son's face. Everybody was amazed by what they saw and congratulated the senior doctor for his work.

After they left, the young doctor was dressing his wound. His father had tears in his eyes. He embraced his son and started sobbing uncontrollably.

'Sorry, my son, I knew what pain you were undergoing during the operation, you never showed it to the public.'

The injection had to be prepared by adding four chemicals, but in his hurry and tension before the operation, the father forgot to add the fourth. Because of that the injection was not at all effective. There was uncontrollable pain during the operation. However the son realized there was something his father had forgotten.

If he showed his pain his father's experiment would fail. He knew how hard his father had worked to develop this medicine. He himself was aware that it was effective. It was unfortunate that something was not making it work now. In the middle of the operation the father too realized the fourth chemical was missing and the medicine was not working. But he was unable to tell this in public. He knew what agony his son was undergoing inspite of the smile on his face. That was why, when everyone left, he broke down crying.

The son consoled his father. 'Father, don't worry. For the welfare of others, I controlled my own pain.'

I don't know how true this story is, but in my sister's and her colleagues' dedication to their work, I thought I saw a glimpse of the sacrifices people in the medical profession make.

A JOURNEY THROUGH DESERT

Till a few years back, I did not have a driver, and used to drive everywhere myself. The petrol bunk where I filled petrol from had a service station beside it. Some Saturdays I would take my car to that service station and stay there until it was serviced. There were two boys, perhaps fourteen years of age, who worked there. They were identical twins. One was called Ram and the other one was Gopal. They were very poor and did not go to school, yet they could speak many languages.

Though Bangalore is the capital of Karnataka, Kannada is not the only language spoken here. There are many people who have come from outside the state and settled in this beautiful city, hence Bangalore has become very cosmopolitan. These boys had met many people during their work in the station and so could speak Kannada, which was their mother tongue, and also Tamil, Telugu and Hindi. Ram and Gopal worked as errand boys. They were always very cheerful and everyone liked them.

The servicing of my car used to take about two hours.

The boys would bring a chair for me and I would sit under the shade of a tree and read some books.

Over a period of time I became friendly with them and they told me about their life. They did not have a father. Their mother worked as a labourer. They stayed in a nearby slum with their uncle. They had studied up to class four but then had to drop out as they were too poor. There was nobody who could guide and teach them at home. Though the salary at the service station was not much, they got free breakfast and lunch and sometimes some small tips from the car owners. They had no fixed working hours. They came around eight in the morning and went home only by 8 p.m. Sundays was the only holiday they got.

In spite of all the difficulties they faced, these kids were always smiling. They never said no or grumbled about any work they were told to do. I have seen children in many well-off families with grumpy faces and no happiness. If you ask them to do any work they give hundreds of reasons to avoid it. I suppose happiness does not depend on the amount of money in the bank.

I used to really like these two boys for their enthusiasm. Once in a while I took snacks and some old shirts for them. They took the clothes with great joy, as if they were made of silk. But I never saw them wear those clothes. If I asked, they said, 'Madam, we always wear dirty clothes to work, because at the station they become greasy.'

Once I took some story books for them, thinking they could read them at night. After all, while other children of their age were studying in schools and attending hockey and chess tournaments, these boys were slogging to make both ends meet. But when I gave them the story books, their faces became pale and for the first time ever I saw a trace of unhappiness on their faces. They said, 'Madam, it takes a lot of time for us to read as we are not used to reading. Will you tell us the story?'

'How can I tell the story here, when you are working all the time?'

'We get some free time at about four o'clock. If you come to service your car then we can sit with you and listen to the story.' Their two pairs of eyes were begging me for the stories and I could not say no. I remembered how my own children always insisted I tell them stories in the night. I agreed.

So it became a routine for me to tell stories on Saturday evenings. I went there even if my car did not need to be serviced. They were very attentive when I told my stories and waited eagerly for more. This went on for many months. Then I decided to get a driver and stopped driving myself. My driver took the car for servicing after that and I did not meet Ram and Gopal for a long time.

Time flows like water. After almost a decade, one day my driver was complaining about some problem the car was giving him. I told him to get it repaired. My old car had outlived its life but was still working. When my driver came back from the garage he said, 'After looking at the car, the car mechanic asked about you. Do you know the owner of the Good Luck Garage?'

'I have not heard this name. Is it a new garage?'

'It is relatively new. I always prefer to go to garages owned by youngsters. This young man is very sincere. It seems he has known you for a long time. He asked if you are still teaching in the college.'

I could not think of anyone I knew who could be owning a garage now. Since my driver did not even know his name, I was unable to place him and assumed it was some old student of mine, though since I teach Computer Science, I could not figure out how this person had shifted to Automobile Engineering. When my driver told me a second time that the owner of the garage had asked about me, I felt I should go and meet this man who was so concerned about me.

The next day I went to the Good Luck Garage. It was a fairly modern garage and well equipped. There was a glass cabin where I assumed the owner was sitting. As soon as I entered, a handsome young man in a blue overall greeted me. He was holding a spanner and a screwdriver in his hand.

'Madam, please come and sit down in the cabin. I will wash my hands and come in a minute.'

I sat on the sofa in his office. It was a nice functional office. The young man looked vaguely familiar to me. I knew I had met him somewhere but could not place where. I wondered, did I teach this boy in pre-university? That time, boys are sixteen or seventeen years old, adolescents with a lot of energy. When I meet them after they have grown up I often fail to recognize them. They look so different and mature. By that time the man had returned with a coffee mug and a glass of water.

'Madam, you have changed a lot. You look old and tired.'

'I am sorry, I am unable to recollect your name. You should excuse me and tell me your name. As you said, I am growing old.'

He smiled at me. There was a dimple on his cheek. And then I knew who he was. He was one of those kids who used to work in the garage a decade back. Was he Ram or Gopal? Even in those days I used to get confused. I asked him, 'Are you Ram or Gopal?'

'I am Ram, Madam.'

'Please sit down. I am very happy to see you like this.'

Now I could understand why Ram had enquired about me after recognizing the car.

'Madam, I am very grateful to you for your help in those days.'

'What help did I give? I used to give some old shirts and eatables and told some stories.'

'Madam, you do not know how your stories changed my life. Do you remember the stories you told us?'

I didn't. From the ocean of stories in my head I had told them a few.

'No, I don't remember.'

He sat down opposite me, closed his eyes and started telling his own story.

'Madam, our life was very difficult. You were aware of it. The only thing we looked forward to was your visit every Saturday when we listened to your stories. We used to stay with our uncle, and whatever we earned he would take. The stories you told us were our only escape from the drudgery of our lives. Our working hours were long. I felt I should go to school and continue my studies. But the night schools were all quite far from where we stayed.

With no financial help or support from home, it seemed studying would always remain a dream, till we heard one of your stories. It made a big difference in our lives.'

Now I was keen to know what happened next.

'Tell me which story was that?' The roles had got reversed. I was the listener and he the storyteller.

'Once, in a village there were many poor people. They all wanted to cross a desert to go to the next village where life was better and the future more promising.

'Many boys wanted to go. The elders in the village had said to them "If you want to do something in life you must go to that town. You pick up stones from the desert and carry to that town. Some buyer will pay money for those rare stones."

'One morning, two boys started their journey. They carried food and water with them. In the beginning, the sand was still cold and the sun not yet hot. Their journey was great. They did not feel tired and strode on. After sometime the sun rose over their heads and the sand started getting hot. After walking for a long time they thought they must have reached the edge of the desert. So they ate all their food and drank the water. But soon they realized they had walked only half the way.

'They also started collecting stones to sell in the town. After some time their bags were full of stones and very heavy. One boy felt it was too much to carry so he threw the stones and decided to go back. The other boy said, "Let us listen to our elders. Come what may, let us cross this desert and go to the next town."

'The first boy did not listen and went back. The second boy continued to walk towards the other town. It was a difficult journey, collecting the stones and travelling all alone, with no water to drink. Sometimes he felt his friend was right. There was no guarantee what was in that town. It was better to stop and go back to the village. But faith and hope kept him going. After walking for a long long time he reached the town. Much to his disappointment, he saw it was like any other town. There was a dharamshala near by. It was getting dark and he was tired. So he decided to spend the night there.

'Next morning, when he got up he wanted to throw away the heavy stones he had collected and return to his village. He opened his bag. What he saw surprised him. All the stones had become big diamonds! In a minute's time he had become a millionaire.

'Do you remember Madam, you also told us the meaning of the story? A student's life is like the desert, examinations are the hot sun, difficulties are like the warm sand and study is like hunger and thirst. As a student you have to travel all alone collecting knowledge and skill the way the boy in the story collected stones. The more you collect the better is the life you lead later.

'After hearing the story I decided to study in spite of all the odds I had to face. With a lot of determination and after facing many difficulties I managed to finish school. The service station owner was also helpful. When I got good marks he helped me pay my fees for an Automobile Diploma. I continued to work while I learnt. Later I took a loan from the bank and started this work. By the grace of God I am successful and have repaid my loan. I am a free person now.

'Madam, rich people are usually scared to start a new

venture. They feel if the venture fails they will lose their money. I never had anything to lose.'

I had learnt this from my own experience too.

'Where is Gopal now?'

'He followed another story of yours.'

Ram looked sad.

'What happened?'

'Gopal's state can also be explained by another story you told us. It seems there was a jackal in the desert. One morning he walked out and faced the sun. He saw his shadow was larger than him. It was so huge that he decided he would hunt a camel for his afternoon meal. He spent the whole day searching for a camel and did not pay attention to the smaller animals he could have caught. He did not find one till the evening. By then his shadow was even smaller than him. So he started hunting for a mouse.

'Gopal was the same. He always tried to do things beyond his capacity and failed miserably. He doesn't even want to work with me. Now he is a peon in an office.'

I was dumbstruck to hear how a small story I had told brought about so much of change. I had never imagined while telling them that such a thing was possible. I am not even the original writer of these stories. I could only silently salute the person who thought of these stories first. Did he or she realize the effect they would have on two children after so many years?

DEAD MAN'S RIDDLE

Often, when there are two or more brothers in a family, they want to divide their parents' property between them and get into arguments and court cases over this.

In the villages, the panchayat decides how the property should be divided. In my childhood, I used to attend meetings of the panchayat with my grandfather where the division of some villager's property would be discussed. The elders would assemble and call the brothers who were fighting for the property. If there were three brothers, they would make three divisions of the property, each of approximately the same value. For example, each part would contain a little bit of gold, some silver and vessels. The values of all the articles in each group would be approximately fixed by the elders of the villages. It was difficult to always make the value of each part equal to the others. In such a situation, the youngest brother would get to choose his part first. The logic behind it was that he had stayed the least number of days with his parents. In those days, in villages, staying with parents was also considered an asset.

The village elders were all well-respected and everyone knew they were impartial. Their decisions were final and no one went to court against them. Going to court for such matters was considered a waste of time and energy. There is a saying in the village that if two feuding parties approach the court, both parties lose money, only the advocate becomes rich.

Once, there was such a disagreement in the division of property of a certain family. The Sarpanch tried his best to make the brothers agree to a certain division but they just would not accept the decision. Finally, Sarpanch Som Gowda told a story which everyone listened to carefully.

It seems, a long time back, in our village itself, there lived a rich man. He had three sons who never agreed with their father about anything. The rich man had a friend called Sumanth, who was well educated and very wise. He would say, time will teach them everything, don't be in a hurry.

One day, the old man died. He left seventeen horses, lots of gold and land for his sons. He wrote a will which was very strange. He divided the land and gold into three parts but for the division of horses there was a riddle. Nobody could understand the riddle. It said, 'The half of the total horses should be given to the elder son, in the remaining half two-third should be given to the second son and what remains out of that two-third should be given to the third son.'

Seventeen was the total number of horses. Half of it meant eight and a half horses to the elder son. That meant one had to kill a horse to divide it. Subsequently, two-third of eight would mean one more horse had to be killed. The old man loved his horses immensely and would never have wanted any of them killed. So what did he mean? The brothers scratched their heads for a few days over the will. When they could not come up with a solution, they showed the will to their father's friend. Sumanth read it and smiled.

He replied, 'It is very easy. Tomorrow morning I will come and divide the horses.'

The next day, everybody assembled in the ground. All seventeen horses were standing in a row. Sumanth came on his own horse. He made his horse stand along with the other horses.

He said, 'Now there are eighteen horses. I am as good as your father. Let us divide the horses as per the will.'

But the sons objected. 'You have added your horse to our horses, that was not our father's wish.'

Sumanth said, 'Don't worry, wait until the division is over. I will take my horse back. Out of these eighteen horses as per the will, half will go the elder son. Half of eighteen is nine, so the elder one gets nine horses. Now there are nine remaining, out of nine two-third means six horses will go the second son. Now there are three remaining. Two-third of three means two horses out of three, will go to the third son. One horse is left, which was any way not yours. It is mine and I am taking it and going home.'

All the people who had assembled were puzzled. The three sons did not know how the division took place without killing a horse. They went to Sumanth and asked, 'Uncle, how did you manage without killing any horse?'

Sumanth smiled and said, 'Experience has taught me many things in life. Your father also knew it. Many a times, a work may look impossible. But if someone gives the smallest suggestion, you can work on it. That is the reason your father wrote his will in such a way that you were forced to take somebody's advice. You may think you know everything, but please remember you are still a student. Life is an eternal teacher, provided you have an open mind.'

Som Gowda concluded, 'That's the way elders have taught us lessons. Experience is the best teacher in life. Elders have seen many ups and downs in their lives and interacted with many people. During the process they have acquired knowledge which can't be taught in a school or college. It has to be learnt over a period of time. Now it is left to you people to make the decision.'

The three brothers, after listening to the story, agreed to the panchayat's division of their property.

'I WILL DO IT'

He was short. He was sharp. He was the brightest boy in his class. His seniors used to ask him to solve their difficulties in science. He could have gone unnoticed in a crowd, but once you asked him a question related to Physics or Maths, there was a spark in his eyes. He could grasp theories of science faster than the speed of light.

He came from a poor but educated family. His father was a high-school teacher and an avid reader of English literature. He, like all the boys in his class, was trying to get admission into some engineering college. The brighter ones wanted to study in the Indian Institutes of Technology, or the IITs. There was an entrance test for IIT. This boy, along with his friends, applied to appear for the test. They did not have any special books or coaching. All these IIT aspirants would sit below the shade of a stone mandap close to Chamundi Hills in the sleepy town of Mysore. He was the guide for the others. While the others struggled to solve the problems in the question paper, he would smile shyly and solve them in no time. He sat alone below a tree and dreamt of studying at IIT. It was the ultimate aim for any bright boy at that age, as it still is today. He was then only sixteen years old.

D-day came. He came to Bangalore, stayed with some relatives and appeared for the entrance test. He did very well but would only say 'ok' when asked. It was the opposite when it came to food. When he said 'ok' it implied 'bad', when he said 'good' it implied 'ok', when he said 'excellent' it implied 'good'. His principle was never to hurt anyone.

The IIT entrance results came. He had passed with a high rank. What a delight for any student! He was thrilled. He went to his father who was reading a newspaper.

'Anna I passed the exam.'

'Well done, my boy.'

'I want to join IIT.'

His father stopped reading the paper. He lifted his head, looked at the boy and said with a heavy voice, 'My son, you are a bright boy. You know our financial position. I have five daughters to be married off and three sons to educate. I am a salaried person. I cannot afford your expenses at IIT. You can stay in Mysore and study as much as you want.'

Indeed it was a difficult situation for any father to say 'no' to his bright son. But circumstances were like that. It was common then for the man to be the single earning member with a large family dependent on him.

His father was sad that he had to tell the bitter truth to his son. But it could not be helped. The boy had to understand reality.

The teenager was disappointed. It seemed his dreams had burnt to ashes. He was so near to fulfilling his fondest hope, yet so far. His heart sank in sorrow.

He did not reply. He never shared his unhappiness or helplessness with anybody. He was an introvert by nature. His heart was bleeding but he did not get angry with anybody.

The day came. His classmates were leaving for Madras, (now Chennai). They were taking a train from Mysore to Madras. They had shared good years in school and college together. He went to the station to say goodbye and good luck to them for their future life.

At the station, his friends were already there. They were excited and talking loudly. The noise was like the chirping of birds. They were all excited and discussing their new hostels, new courses etc. He was not part of it. So he stood there silently. One of them noticed and said, 'You should have made it.'

He did not reply. He only wished all of them. They waved at him as the train slowly left the platform.

He stood there even after he could no longer see the train or the waving hands. It was the June of 1962 in Mysore city. Monsoon had set in and it was getting dark. It had started to drizzle. Yet he stood there motionless.

He said to himself, without anger or jealousy, 'All students from the IITs study well and do big things in life. But it is not the institution, ultimately it is you and you alone who can change your life by hard work.'

Probably he was not aware that he was following the

philosophy of the Bhagavad Gita: 'Your best friend is yourself and your worst enemy is yourself.'

Later he worked very hard, and focused on one thing, never bothering about his personal life or comforts. He shared his wealth with others. He never used the help of any caste, community or political connections to go up in life.

A son of a schoolteacher showed other Indians it was possible to earn wealth legally and ethically. He built a team of people who were equally good.

He became a pioneer of India's software industry and started the Information Technology wave. Today he has become an icon of simplicity, uncompromising quality and fairness, apart from being a philanthropist. He really believes in the motto, 'Powered by intellect and driven by values'.

He is none other than Infosys founder and present Chairman, Nagavara Ramarao Narayana Murthy.

THE RAINY DAY

When I was young, before a girl got married, her mother would give her some words of advice. They were usually like: 'You must adjust to your new house and in-laws, try to learn how they eat and cook their food, go out of your way to be friendly and helpful to everybody,' etc.

My mother, Vimala Kulkarni, told me similar words when I got married. But along with this, she said something which helped me immensely in later life. She said, 'In life we never know when a rainy day will come and you might fall short of money. In order to be prepared for such a situation, you should always save some money from your salary, and if you are not earning, then from your husband's salary. If your salary is one thousand rupees take fifty or hundred rupees and keep it separately. This money should not be used for buying ornaments or silk saris. When you are young, you want to spend money and buy many things but remember, when you are in difficulty only few things will come to your help. Your courage, your ability to adjust to new situations and the money which you have saved. Nobody will come and help you.'

When I heard her advice I laughed. I felt it was impossible that such a 'rainy day' would ever come in my life. I was young and thought every day was a sunny day. But I always listened to my mother, so I started saving slowly. The money was kept in a safe place in my kitchen cupboard and I never counted it.

After my marriage, for a while life was smooth in Bombay. We had a daughter and were happy like any other middle class family. We used to stay in a flat in Bandra. I used to work for TELCO at Fort and Murthy for PCS at Nariman Point.

One day, my husband returned from office looking very worried. By nature he is not talkative and is reluctant to share his emotions, but that day he was different. I was making some chapattis in the kitchen.

'Why are you looking so worried?' I asked him.

He replied, 'Software is going to be the biggest new business in the years to come. We have no dearth of intelligent people in our country. Writing software requires a logical mind and hard work, which we can find plenty of in India. I feel I should harness this talent. I want to start a software company.'

I was shocked. I had never imagined we would ever think of starting our own company. Both in my family and Murthy's there was not a single person who was an entrepreneur. I had thought Murthy will work in PCS and

My immediate reaction was 'No'.

Murthy started explaining his plans and vision for the business to me. 'You are fond of history. You must appreciate my reasoning. You know we Indians missed the Industrial Revolution. That time we were ruled by foreigners. Now the world is on the threshold of an intellectual revolution. We must make full use of this. We have to bring this revolution to our country. If we miss this we shall never get a chance to do well in life. I want to take this step not for money alone. This is one desire that I have had for a while now. Let me do it now. It is now or never.'

My mind went back to my childhood days. One of our relatives had started something on his 'own'. He ended up incurring heavy losses. Finally he had to sell his family property. So for me, starting our own business was synonymous with loss. I was afraid the same thing would happen to us. We did not even have any property to sell in order to cover our loss. Apart from that, we had a daughter now. I was confused.

Probably Murthy read my mind. He said, 'This is a new kind of industry. It is driven by intellect and does not require large capital. I need your wholehearted support.'

There was sincerity and honesty in his voice. I have always respected and appreciated his honesty.

As I sat there wondering what was right, I smelt the chapattis burning in the kitchen. The smell reminded me that we would have to have our dinner without chapattis that day.

Still I sat and measured the odds and consequences of the problem. Murthy had a large family and they were dependent on him. He had unmarried sisters. In such a situation, if he started a new company our financial stability would be severely affected. I was worried, but I also had a lot of faith in him. I felt that unless I supported him wholeheartedly, he would feel uncomfortable starting a new venture like this. In business there is always profit and loss. If we went into a loss, we would lose our precious savings of many years. Yet, when I thought about it, in my heart, I was also sure that we would survive somehow.

I asked him, 'Are you alone in this?'

Murthy rarely smiles. This time he smiled and replied, 'No, six of my young colleagues are joining me. This is our one chance to earn money legally and ethically. I have a dream that India should be a leader in this industry which will bring pride and revenue to our country. You have to help me. Can you give me some money? If you don't help me now my dream will remain unfulfilled.'

I knew that if I did not give him the money he would not be able to start his company. At that moment I remembered my mother's words. 'Save some money and use it only in extremely essential situations.' This was one of those situations. Finally I came to a decision. I went inside the kitchen and opened my rainy day saving box. I took out the money I had deposited in it every month and counted. There were ten thousand rupees. I took it, offered up a brief prayer to God and gave it to Murthy.

'All the best Murthy, that's all I can give you. With happiness I will bear all the responsibilities of this new enterprise. By the way, what are you going to name this company?'

'Infosys, and thank you for your support and the seed money. Be ready for the most bumpy ride in your life for the next few years.'

When I look back now, I realize that our lives changed completely because I had listened to my mother's valuable lesson.

I often tell this story to my children and students. One never knows when a rainy day will come. And when it does, my mother's words will always stay true.

DOING WHAT YOU LIKE IS FREEDOM

One day, I was travelling by train from Bangalore to Belgaum. It is an overnight train and the only rail link between Bangalore and north Karnataka. I was travelling by second class as that's where one can meet lots of people who are eager to talk. I have noticed, the more expensive the ticket, the lesser the co-travellers speak.

As I settled down in my seat, I glanced at the opposite berth. There was a small family of husband, wife and son. The son was about eighteen or nineteen years old and probably going to college. The family was obviously quite well-off. I sat and watched them. The parents were giving numerous instructions to their son.

'It is very cold, why don't you wear a sweater?'

'Are you hungry? Shall I serve food?'

'We have got three berths, lower, middle and upper, which one would you want to take?'

'Have you brought your bathroom slippers? If you are going to the bathroom please use them...' and so on.

The young boy looked ill at ease at all their attention, particularly in front of a stranger, but was obeying and answering them reluctantly.

Then the father asked the mother, 'Did you bring some old cloth? I want to clean these seats. They look dirty.'

The mother answered, 'How many times have I told you to make reservations early. But you never listen to me. If you had booked the tickets earlier, we could have gone by first class or second AC. People like us travel in those compartments and they are maintained better, not like this second class where every Tom, Dick and Harry travels.'

The father bowed his head and answered, 'Nowadays there's so much rush for tickets for the higher classes. I did not realize that. Normally we travel by air so I underestimated the situation. Unfortunately this Belgaum does not have an air connection.'

By now, since I knew they were also travelling up to Belgaum and we were going to be together till eight o'clock the next morning, I struck up a conversation with them.

'Are you going to Belgaum for the first time?'

They looked at me with some surprise, but the woman was eager to talk.

'Yes, we have never gone there before. My son has got admission in the Belgaum Medical College. We have heard it is a good college. Do you know anything about it?'

'Yes, it is a good college.'

'How do you know?'

'Because I belong to that area.'

After this they were eager to talk to me as they wanted to know more about the town.

The man introduced himself. 'I am Rao. I am a CA in Bangalore. This is my wife Ragini. She is an MA in Home Science. That's my son Puneet, who is going to be a medical student.' He gave me his card.

By now the train had started moving. Even before it left Bangalore city, they had opened their dinner box. It was a huge tiffin carrier and many items were placed in it. The mother laid table mats on the berth and placed steel plates. It was as if she was serving dinner at home. There were two subjis, two kinds of dal, roti, rice and a dessert. It was an eight-course meal! I watched them in amazement. The son sat down quietly for his meal but before he could touch his plate his mother said, 'Take the Dettol soap, wear your bathroom slippers, carry this towel, wash your hands and come for dinner.'

When he left, his father explained to me, 'Puneet is our only son. We have brought him up very well. We wanted him to study medicine in some college in Bangalore but unfortunately he got admission in Belgaum. We have never sent him alone anywhere. This is the first time we are leaving him. We were thinking if the hostel does not suit him my wife will shift to Belgaum and we will rent a small house there for the next five years. I will stay in Bangalore and meet them once a week. For children's sake parents have to make sacrifices.' His voice broke and I could see tears in the lady's eyes.

I could understand their pain at their only son leaving home. It is always a difficult time for parents, but it is also inevitable. How long can you keep birds in cages when their wings are strong and they are ready to fly? We can give our children only two things in life which are essential. Strong roots and powerful wings. Then they may fly anywhere and live independently. Of all the luxuries in life, the greatest luxury is getting freedom of the right kind.

Now the mother joined in. They were clearly very upset and worried. They wanted to share their grief with somebody, even though I was unknown to them.

'Our son is very dear to us. I was a lecturer in a college, but I left my job after his birth. Many of my colleagues have become Principals in other colleges but I was determined to bring up my son very well.'

The husband said, 'I had a good practice in Tumkur district and I own plenty of land there but I decided to shift to Bangalore for Puneet's studies. I visit my farm once in a while. I bought an apartment next to his school. I don't go anywhere without my family.'

'I take his lunch to school every day. Then I talk to his teacher regarding his performance. I have also enrolled him in different evening classes. He learns chess as it is good for the brain, karate to protect himself and cricket which is a well-respected game.'

I could not control my laughter. I felt pity for the child. I asked, 'What about music, general knowledge, debating?'

'Oh, we don't require all these. When he was born we decided he should become a doctor.'

'What is his choice?'

'Our choice is his choice. He is only a child. What does

he know about the outside world?'

By that time the 'child' came and they started eating their dinner. After finishing, the parents decided he should sleep on the lower berth. Immediately a bed was made by the father. He spread a snow white bedsheet, an air pillow and the boy was made to lie down and covered with a Kashmiri shawl.

'I hope you don't mind, we want to switch off the lights. My son cannot sleep with the lights on.'

The gentleman switched off the light without even waiting for my reply. I was left sitting alone without dinner and not feeling in the least sleepy.

I was wondering what Puneet's mother will do when he gets married. They seemed to have forgotten that he was an independent person who could take his own decisions with some love and guidance. Instead, they were bombarding him with their own ideas and opinions. Too much of affection can become a golden noose around the neck. Puneet will never be a confident person.

It was only ten in the night. I never sleep that early. Even in the partial darkness I spotted an old friend walking down the passage. We were delighted to meet each other so unexpectedly.

'Come on, why are you sitting in the dark?' she asked. 'Are you planning to steal somebody's purse? How can you sleep at ten o'clock? Come to my compartment. It is the next one. Let us talk for some time. It is very hard to catch you in Bangalore.' She started laughing loudly at her own joke.

A quiet conversation in north Karnataka would mean

a high-pitched talk in sophisticated society.

'I have reservation only for this compartment.'

'Don't worry, we will tell the ticket collector. In my compartment one berth is vacant.' My loyalty switched immediately and I followed her.

There was loud laughter and joking going on in the other compartment. My other friends were also there. We sat and remembered our college days and made fun of each other.

In the midst of us middle-aged people there was a young boy sitting. He too was very jolly with enormous energy. When all of us opened our tiffin boxes, the boy offered everyone bananas from his bag. Though he did not know any of us he looked confident and happy.

I asked him, 'What is your name? Where are you going?'

'My name is Sharad. I am going to Belgaum.'

'Why are you going there?'

'I have got a seat in the medical college there and I am going to join my class.'

'Are you going for the first time? Do you have anybody with you?'

'Yes, I am going for the first time and I am alone.'

I forgot my tiffin box. Suddenly I thought of Puneet who was of the same age as this boy.

'Where are your parents?'

'My father is a postman and my mother is a schoolteacher. I come from a village near Kolar.'

'How many siblings do you have?'

'I am the only child.'

'Did you never get lonely?'

'No. Since both my parents were working I knew all the neighbours. After school I would visit one house every day. All those children I used to visit became like my brothers and sisters.'

I wanted to know what all subjects he studied in school.

'My father being a postman, I learnt cycling at a very young age. In the evenings I did some extra curricular activities. My father always told me "in life extremes are bad". It is better if one takes the middle path so one should know a little bit of music, sports, social activities. This helped me a lot. Now I can travel anywhere without a problem because I know four languages: English, Kannada, Hindi and Telugu. I can swim, sing. I was in NCC so I travelled to many places with my batch.'

'How did you do in your exam?'

'I think I did fairly well. I got a seat in Belgaum Medical College didn't I.'

'Is it not very expensive?'

'It is expensive. My parents have sacrificed a lot and I have taken a bank loan. I am confident I will repay the loan once I start working.'

'Tell me, for a young person, what do you think is the most important thing?'

'It is freedom. Freedom to choose your own life; freedom to pursue your own interest; freedom to enjoy your own likes, provided they are not harmful to you and the society. I feel I was very fortunate to grow up with so much of freedom, like a tree in the forest.'

Somehow, I felt I had seen a stunted bonsai plant in the previous compartment.

GOWRAMMA'S LETTER

In India, particularly in villages, even a few decades back, women without children were looked down upon. Such women were not invited for naming ceremonies, and were taunted as barren women. Nobody understood the hurt and trauma they underwent.

When I was a child, I had a teacher called Gowramma. She was kind and warm. She was also tall, beautiful and always cheerful. She used to teach us Sanskrit. She was a great teacher and would tell lots of stories in the class. Students usually took Sanskrit as an optional language, in order to score marks like Maths. They were not interested in the story. They only wanted to get good grades and were not interested in Gowramma's old epics. As soon as the class was over, students used to run to escape from her elaborate stories. But I always loved listening to stories, so I would sit with her for hours.

Storytelling is an art which not everyone is good at.

There are many ways to tell a story. You have to change your voice depending on the circumstance, and describe people you have never seen.

Gowramma described Lord Krishna as a tall, handsome person with a dark complexion, a mischievous smile and a kind heart. Later when I saw Mahabharata on TV, the actor who was playing Krishna's role was exactly how she had described. Whereas when I saw Ramayana on TV, the actor looked very different from what I had imagined Lord Rama to be like. The storyteller influences your imagination of what the characters in the story looked like.

Gowramma would pick up many stories from Katha Sarithsagara, literally meaning the ocean of stories, and recreate the scenes for me. For us time would stop and we would be immersed in the story until the peon of the school would come and harshly tell us, 'Time is up. Except you two only the school ghost is here. You may not be scared of the ghost but I am. Kindly vacate the room.'

Then Gowramma and I would get up and depart with a heavy heart.

This went on till I was in class seven. Then I joined another school. For a few days I missed Gowramma, but soon I forgot her in my new activities. Once in a while I met her at the market place and she would affectionately ask about my studies.

At home, whenever I got lost in a storybook, I would be teased as Gowramma's only true student. My mother would tell me sadly, 'Poor Gowramma, she is so beautiful, so good-natured but luck is not on her side. Her husband has left her because she cannot bear a child. He has married another woman. That woman has produced children but in no other way is she a match to Gowramma.' Then I would understand the reason behind the sadness in Gowramma's eyes.

Time flew by as swift and light as straw. I did my Engineering, got married, had children and later became the Chairperson of Infosys Foundation. I toured the length and breadth of the country, met many celebrities and many poor people. My life became public.

I was often invited to colleges and universities to deliver lectures. Once, I went to a university to deliver a lecture. After it was over, students gathered to ask some questions. Though it was getting late for my next programme, since I love talking to students, I remained there answering their questions. I feel students are like my young friends, brighter than me but with less experience.

Students also ask me a lot of questions about my young days so that they can relate to my life.

One bright girl in the crowd asked me a question which left me dazed. It was a most difficult question. 'When you are faced with some difficulty, how do you solve it? Do you avoid it?'

I did not know how to answer her and was tempted to ignore her but my heart would not let me do that. She was a girl of twenty years, bright and simple, direct and bold with no hesitation or shyness. When she saw me looking at her blankly, she repeated the same question. Somehow, looking at her, I felt I was looking at myself when I was twenty years old.

In a fraction of a second an answer came to my mind. 'Children, in answer to this question, I will tell you a story. It is a story from the Ramayana. In the battlefield at Lanka, during the battle between Rama, Lakshmana and Ravana, Lakshmana became unconscious. He needed the medicine plant Sanjeevini to revive. Sanjeevini was only available in the Dhrona mountains. These mountains were huge and far away. The only person who could do this job was Hanumana. Hanumana flew to Dhrona mountains, but alas, he was unable to recognize which was the Sanjeevini plant. Time was running short. The only way out was to take the entire mountain along with the plants to Rama. The mountain was huge, how could he lift it? But Hanumana had the gift to increase his body size. He became higher than the mountain, till it was like a pebble for him. Then he put the mountain on his palm and flew back to Lanka. The rest of the story all of you know.'

The girl was impatient and restless.

She said, ' I asked you a different question but you told me an old story which everyone knows.'

I smiled at her and said, 'Have patience. I have not yet completed my answer. When you come across difficulties, you have to grow bigger than the problem. You have that capacity within you, but you are not aware of it. If you become bigger, difficulties will look smaller than you, and you can solve them easily. If you become smaller than the difficulties, they will look like mountains and crush you. This is the theory I have followed in life.'

The students were pleased with my answer and there

was a lot of applause. I stopped them in the middle of the clapping, with moist eyes and a heavy voice, 'The credit for this answer should go to my teacher Gowramma. When I was young she taught me this lesson. She used to tell me many ancient stories which are priceless in their wisdom. To understand them we need great storytellers like Gowramma. It was she who taught me to love stories when I was young.'

The function got over and I returned to Bangalore. As usual I became busier than ever. I forgot about the whole thing.

One day there was a letter. My secretary came up to me and said, 'Madam, it seems to be from somebody who knows you well. Probably this is a personal letter, so I did not read it.' She placed the letter in front of me and left. I was wondering who it could be from. It was written in a shaky handwriting. I looked closely at the name at the bottom and was surprised. It was from Gowramma.

It said, 'I think you know my husband left me long back and everyone used to make fun of me and call me a "barren woman". Everyone looked down on me and called me story teacher rather than Sanskrit teacher. Sometimes people used to tell me that instead of telling stories to children I should make money by giving private tuition classes. I did not, because I believed in my work. I was always humiliated because I could not bear any children. You know my husband married a second time and had his own children. These children got into bad habits and brought shame and debt to him. He used to come and cry at my doorsteps. At that time I helped him with my savings . . .'

I could not understand why Gowramma had written this personal story to me. I was aware of her situation. But why had she written it all to me now? But patience is one quality I have acquired along with my grey hair. It told me to complete reading the letter.

'Today my husband brought me the newspaper and showed it to me. He said that you mentioned my name in public and contributed your success to my storytelling. For a minute I was frozen. I am not your biological mother but you behaved as if you were my child. People have children, but they fight and bring disgrace and shame to their parents. My husband felt ashamed about his own children, whereas I felt proud about my child whom I taught selflessly and who listened wholeheartedly. You made me proud. Now I don't have any complaint with God.'

Tears welled up in my eyes and fell on the letter mingling with the ink. I was unable to read further.

WHO IS GREAT?

Whenever I teach my class, I make sure that everyone participates in the question-answer session. I normally teach for forty minutes and the last twenty minutes I keep open for debates, questions and answers. This way, students learn to express their opinions in front of others and the teacher also understands how much the students have learnt. Many times I have learnt a lot from my students during these sessions. Sometimes their questions are so difficult I am not able to answer. Then I tell them that I will refer to my books and answer the next day.

Frequently, after the class I tell a story which leads to debates. Once, I made a statement, 'Many a times there is no perfect solution for a given problem. No solution is also a solution. Everything depends upon how you look at it. We make judgements on others depending upon what we think of them.'

My students immediately objected to this statement.

'Convince us,' they said.

'Okay, I will tell you a simple story. This happened many centuries back. There was a beautiful girl called Rathnaprabha who was rich and bright. She completed her studies and asked her teacher, "What shall I pay you as *gurudakshina*?"'

'Her teacher replied, "Your father has already paid me. You don't have to worry."'

'Rathnaprabha insisted and the teacher was upset. He said to himself, "I want to test the courage of this girl. Let me put a difficult condition which she will not be able to fulfil. Then she will not trouble me any more."'

'So he said, "Rathnaprabha, on a moonless night you should deck yourself with lots of jewellery and come to my house all alone."'

'There was a forest between Rathnaprabha's house and the teacher's. The road was very bad. There were many animals in the forest and a river too. Rathnaprabha thought for a minute and went away. The teacher was very happy that he had silenced his student.

'Finally it was a moonless night. Rathnaprabha decked herself with expensive jewellery and was about to set out to her teacher's house. Her father saw this and was very upset. He asked her where she was going, so Rathnaprabha narrated the story. Her father was taken aback.

'He said, "Your teacher is a nice person, you must have troubled him, which is why he told you to do this, just to teach you a lesson. I know him well, I will explain to him tomorrow. Don't go. He will understand and he will pardon you. You are like a daughter to him."

'Rathnaprabha did not listen. She insisted on going all alone as she had promised she would. There were many animals in the forest but she had made up her mind and kept walking.

'Suddenly, she was stopped by a young thief. He had never seen so many expensive ornaments and was delighted by the amount of money he would make that night. He stopped her and told her his intentions.

'Rathnaprabha was unperturbed. She said, "I promised my teacher I would go to him wearing all these ornaments. I will give them to you when I come back from my teacher's house. I always keep my word."

'The thief was surprised and let her go. But he followed her secretly to know what happened next. Rathnaprabha knocked on the door of the teacher's house. He opened the door and was surprised and sad to see her.

'"I thought you would take it as a joke. It was only to discourage you. I never thought you would come here against all the odds. Please go back home. I will bless you my child. You are a woman of your word."

'Rathnaprabha turned to go back when the thief appeared before her. She said to him, "I promised to give you all my ornaments. Please take them."

'The thief smiled and said, "You are an unusual woman. I don't want anything from you. It is difficult to meet people like you."

'Rathnaprabha came home. Her father was waiting at the doorstep. She described everything to him. Her father was proud and happy. He said, "You are courageous and you kept your word. Come inside and take rest. You have travelled a lot today."'

When I completed the story, my students were not impressed. They said, 'What is great in this story? There is a headstrong girl, a foolish teacher, an impractical thief and an irresponsible father. What do we have to learn from this story?'

I told them, 'That is how you view things. I understand the story in a different way. Courageous Rathnaprabha, kind-hearted teacher, generous thief and a responsible father who values his daughter's words. Who do you think was the greatest person in the story?'

A lot of noise broke out in the classroom. The students started debating and arguing amongst themselves. I was smiling and looking at them.

One group got up and said, 'Madam, we think Rathnaprabha was great because she was aware of all the difficulties and yet did not change her mind. She was opposed by her father, scared by the thief, worried about the animals in the forest, but still she believed that *gurudakshina* should be given to her teacher. We only hope Madam, you will not ask such a *gurudakshina* from us.' The whole class burst into laughter. I did not answer.

Another group immediately got up and argued, 'We don't agree. There was nothing great about Rathnaprabha. She was a headstrong girl. The thief was the greatest person because a thief usually robs people without asking their victims or worrying about what happened to them afterwards. There is some bond between the teacher and Rathnaprabha and between

Rathnaprabha and her father. They had some commitment to each other whereas the thief was not a part of the system. So we think the thief was the greatest personality.'

Before they could complete, another group got up and argued for the teacher. 'The teacher was the greatest. He told Rathnaprabha not to worry about the fees. But when she was adamant, he put forth a difficult condition. When she came he was surprised and worried. He did not ask anything else. He blessed her wholeheartedly.'

The last group did not agree, because they believed the father was the greatest. They argued, 'The father allowed Rathnaprabha to take her own decision. How many fathers even today allow their daughters to do that? Madam, in this class how many girls can take independent decisions?'

Things became too noisy after this because the debate had now become personal. I realized it was time for me to interfere.

I said, 'There is no one person in this story who was great. It is the way we look at it. Similarly, whenever any problem arises we should view it from different angles. The decisions each of us arrive at will be different. Whenever we blame somebody, for a minute we should enter into that person's mind and try to understand why he did what he did. Only then should we take a decision.'

Now my entire class agreed with me.

BALU'S STORY

Balu is my cousin. In no way is he extraordinary, yet he is very special to me. That is because he can always see the lighter side of any situation, however difficult. When I talk to him I feel life is so simple, and I have been complicating it unnecessarily.

Once, a friend of mine who was working in a bank, was transferred to a small village in a forest area. He was worried about his family, children, their education, etc. He could not resign, as he would not have got another job at that age. One day, while he had come to my house and was telling me his worries, Balu came. He heard the problem and started laughing.

'If I were you I would have accepted this happily. You can leave your children with your parents. Grandparents always look after children very well and also teach them better lessons. Is it not true, Sudha?' Without waiting for my answer, he continued, 'Of late your health has not been good. In this city it is difficult to go for a walk. The congestion and traffic chokes your throat. The best cure for your problems is to go for a five-kilometre walk every day. How will you do that here? That is why a village is the best place for you. There are trees everywhere and the air is fresh. Take advantage of this situation and enjoy it. Your wife can visit you once a month and you can come here once, that means you will meet your family twice a month. Sometimes it is better to be away from the family for a while, as you get a lot more respect. This is my personal experience.' Balu finished in a hushed tone.

My friend certainly looked more at ease after listening to Balu's speech. That is the way Balu speaks. If somebody fails in the exam, Balu has a readymade consolation.

'In life, some failures are essential. Repeated success makes a person arrogant, whereas occasional failures are essential to become mature. Have you not heard the famous words, "Try and try and try again, you will succeed at last." Don't fail next time. Start studying now.'

Parents don't always like this advice of his but it goes down very well with the students.

Another cousin of mine, Prasad, is always complaining, 'People cheat me a lot. I want to help everybody, but people take advantage of me.'

Balu was ready with a clever answer, 'There was a person who used to complain the whole day, from morning to evening, that he had a headache, a stomach ache or a leg pain. I asked him, "Show me where you are aching." He pointed all over his body with a finger. Then I told him, "You have a pain in your finger and not in the other parts of the body." Prasad, when you say everyone is cheating you and taking advantage of you, then you have a problem, not others.'

Balu is a good narrator and once he starts describing something he forgets the time. That is the reason why he is very popular with children.

He exaggerates his stories, is never punctual, but still I enjoy his company. He is not cunning and would never hurt anyone. He can live without food but not without talking.

His children have all grown up now and done well in life. Balu jokes about this too. 'They have done well because I did not help them in studies.' He can laugh as much at himself as at others.

Balu has travelled to many places. He has a story to tell about every place he has visited, but I usually take them with a pinch of salt. His son works in the US. When he had a baby, he invited his parents to the US for a year. Before Balu left, the whole village knew he was going abroad. After he came back, he summoned everyone in the village under the big banyan tree and said, 'I want to describe my experiences in the US.'

Today, going abroad is not anything great. But not too many people from our village had gone. The ones who had gone did not describe their stay there in too many details. They just said, 'That is a different country with a different value system.'

But Balu was not like that. He started describing his stay endlessly from the day he arrived. I knew Balu's nature, so before he went to tell all the villagers his stories under the banyan tree, I said to him, 'You don't have control on your tongue. Anybody can make out that you are telling a lie. There is a method to describe and a limit to exaggeration. If you want to tell some boy is tall you can say he is perhaps six feet four inches in height. But you will say, the boy is ten feet tall, which is not possible. People make fun of you. Do not underestimate villagers. They know about America. They have seen it on TV.'

Balu did not argue. He said, 'I agree. But when I start talking I lose control over my tongue. Exaggeration has become a habit with me. Will you do me a favour? When I start exaggerating you pull my shirt. Then I will understand and I will correct myself immediately.'

We agreed. Balu started describing New York City with its tall buildings. But one of the villagers got up and said, 'We have seen this city many times on TV after September 11th. Don't exaggerate. Tell us something about their methods of agriculture, their fodder, grass etc. Then we can compare them to our ways.'

Balu said, 'Oh, I saw their fields and the grass. The grass was almost five feet tall.'

I pulled his shirt.

He realized he was talking too much. Immediately he said, 'No, no, the grass is very thin.'

Somebody asked, 'What do you mean very thin?'

'It was as thin as a hair's width.'

Again I pulled his shirt. But I was so exasperated that I pulled it very hard and it tore. Balu, for once, did not know what to say. But I could hear people talking, 'After all, it is Balu's version of America. The real America must be different.'

Balu's wife is very quiet, which is understandable. If

two people talk too much it can get difficult to live together. Once she was unwell and had a very high fever. Balu talks a lot, but in such a situation he gets scared easily. He was very worried and called me up.

'Get a doctor immediately. My wife is running a very high temperature.'

'What do you mean by very high temperature. How much is it?'

'Oh, it must be about five hundred degrees.'

'Then you should not call a doctor, you better call a fire fighter. Kindly check with the thermometer. It must not be more than 106 degrees.'

Once we were sitting and chatting when a stranger entered. Many people are aware that Infosys Foundation helps students to study further if they do not have the funds. With help from the Foundation, many children have graduated and stood on their own feet. Whenever I am in villages, parents of such children come and see me. After talking to them, if I feel the case is genuine, we help them. This stranger came with a similar request.

I had a detailed talk with him and was convinced his son needed help.

I told him, 'After I go back to my office I will send you the cheque.'

Balu called me aside and said, 'How can you say that? Do you know what may happen tomorrow? Will you remember your promise? There is a gap between today evening and tomorrow morning. Life is uncertain; anything can happen. If you want to give anything, you must give him immediately. Time is never in your hands. On the contrary, all of us are living at the mercy of time.'

'Balu, I don't have a cheque book with me.'

'That is your mistake. You must carry a cheque book and cash when you travel for this purpose. Many times poor people may not even have an account in the post office or bank.'

I always thought Balu was only an uneducated, hilarious, comic man. But I was wrong. He taught me a great lesson. When donating don't think twice, or put it off for another day. Nobody has conquered time. Time is not in anybody's hand.

'A' FOR HONESTY

The American education system at the university level is different from ours. There, the final marks are based on the average marks of three examinations held earlier in the semester. As a result, students have to study and do well consistently, and there is not much pressure during the final exam. There is also greater student-teacher interaction in that system.

As a teacher, I have seen that sometimes even a bright student may not do well because of the pressures of the final test. There are other ways to examine the depth of knowledge of the student, like surprise exams, open book exams, oral exams etc. The examination should not scare the students, instead it should measure their knowledge fairly and give marks accordingly. This kind of system requires more number of teachers for students. However, this is difficult to achieve in India, where there are large numbers of students. There is also great pressure on students from the parents and society to perform well.

My son is studying in a college in the US. He loves Computer Science immensely and always puts in a lot of hard work when he studies it. One day, he called me after his mid-term exams. I could make out from his voice that he was very sad. He told me, 'I did not do my exams well. It is not that I did not know the answers, but instead of digit eight I assumed the digit as six and did the entire calculation based on that. I prepared so well and now I know I will not do well. I'm feeling very depressed.'

As a teacher, I don't give too much of importance to marks because I am aware of such situations. Many a time I have seen children who are really good in subjects unable to answer questions due to various factors. So I consoled him.

'Don't worry. So what? You have lost the battle but you will win the war. Examinations are not the only index in life. Keep courage, face reality and don't be negligent while reading the questions. Good luck for next time.'

He was not at all pleased to hear my words. 'You talk like a moral science teacher, Amma. It is very competitive here and difficult to achieve anything in such an atmosphere. You are a teacher and you only give grades. You don't sit for the exams. So you do not know the difficulties of students.'

I knew he was sad. My consolation did not help him. But he had forgotten that once upon a time I was also a student and had passed through the same passage.

After few days, I got another call from him. There was joy and great enthusiasm in his voice. Suddenly the dark winter days had turned into bright sunny days.

'Amma, you know I got grade "A" in that subject, which I did not do well.'

'How come?' I was very surprised.

'It is a very funny thing. After the exam I was talking to the professor and we were discussing various topics. When I got my papers I saw I had got good marks for the question which I had answered wrongly. My other friends said the professor must have made a mistake, don't tell him, keep quiet. Getting a good grade is more important in this competitive world.'

'What did you do?' I asked anxiously.

'I thought for a while, then I realized, grades are important but honesty is even more important. You taught me that when I was a little boy. Do you remember, Amma? Once the shopkeeper mistook fifty rupees as one hundred rupees and gave the change for one hundred. At that time we did not have much money, but still you sent me back to the shop to return the extra money. At that age I was so reluctant to go and return the change but you were strict with me and said if I didn't, I would have to go without dinner. Somehow I was unable to keep quiet about the professor's mistake. I wrote an email to him saying I did not deserve those marks. But his reply was more surprising.'

'What was that?'

'He replied, "I have not given the marks by mistake. It was deliberate. After the exams I was talking to you, and my constant interaction with you throughout the semester had convinced me of the depth of your knowledge and your passion for the subject. Mistakes do happen by oversight or due to tension. That is the reason I gave you some marks for that question. After all, exams should also measure the depth of your knowledge.'"

My eyes filled with tears on hearing this story. I was happy not because he had got an 'A' grade but because he had practised what he believed in. Many of my own students have behaved in a similar way in different situations, though they may have lost a lot in the process. To some people it may seem to be stupidity. But I am sure the good values they have learnt will help them in any crisis.

A LESSON IN INGRATITUDE

I was attending a seminar on how to eliminate poverty. For some reason, such seminars always seem to be held in five-star hotels. I really do not know why they have to be organized in the most expensive places.

After attending the seminar, I was standing in the lobby of the hotel, when I saw a middle-aged person in an Armani suit with a pipe in his hand. His perfume was expensive and very strong. I could smell it from a considerable distance. He was talking on his mobile and was probably waiting for his car. I looked at him and felt sure I had seen him somewhere earlier. He finished his call and stared at me. Both of us were trying to place each other. Suddenly I realized he was my classmate from thirty years back. His name was Suresh. I said, 'Are you Suresh? Who was my classmate ...'

He said, 'I was wondering, are you Sudha?'

We started laughing. It was over thirty years since we

had last met. Both of us had put on weight and become different to look at from our college days. Suresh and I went to the same college, where we knew each other fairly well for four years. We attended many lab classes together where he was my lab partner.

I asked him, 'I have not met you for a long time. The last I heard you were in Bombay. What are you doing here?'

'Yes, I live in Bombay. I have my own business there. By the grace of God I am doing very well. Why don't we meet up sometime and talk about the old days? By the way, where are you going? Can I drop you?'

I agreed immediately because my driver was on leave. By then his Mercedes Benz car had arrived at the hotel door and we got into the car.

Suresh started explaining. 'I own a few companies in Bombay and Bangalore. I am into Medical Transcription. I also train people and send them abroad for software jobs. Now there is a dearth of teachers in UK. I want to train teachers and send them. This is a very lucrative job as there are not many overheads... I heard from many people you have become a teacher and a social worker. I felt sad for you. You would have done well in business. You were one of the brightest in the class.'

He looked genuinely sad at my choice of profession. To console him I said, 'Don't look so sad. I took up this profession out of choice not compulsion. Do you know Suresh, "Doing what you like is freedom, liking what you do is happiness." If you look at it that way, I am very happy.'

By then we had reached my office. Before I got off the car, Suresh gave me his visiting card and insisted I come to his house for dinner or breakfast.

One Sunday I was free and I remembered Suresh's invitation. I called up his home and his secretary told me he was in Bombay. She fixed up a breakfast for the next Sunday. She also said she would send a car to pick me up as it was difficult to locate the house.

That Sunday morning, a driver came with a Toyota car and I left. I started chatting with the driver after some time. He was very talkative as he knew I was his boss's classmate. Suresh's house was sixty kilometres away from Bangalore city. It was a farmhouse on the banks of the river Cauvery. It was inside a forest and spread over twenty acres of land. There they grew fruits and vegetables without using chemical fertilizers. Madam, the driver told me, is very conscious about health and has got a special gym and a swimming pool made. Suresh had another house in Indiranagar, in the heart of Bangalore city. They visited this farm only on weekends and invited special guests there.

I asked him, 'How long have you been working for Suresh?'

'Oh, I have been with him for the last twenty years. Actually I was his father-in-law's driver. He was a businessman in Bombay, and Madam his only daughter. I can call Madam by her first name if I want to, I have known them for that long, but I don't do that.'

I could make out a sense of belonging and a shade of pride on the driver's face.

When I reached the house, I realized the driver had not exaggerated in his description of the place. It was like entering a palace. There were five or six guest rooms, a huge hall, a large dining room, spacious courtyards, all built in the traditional Indian style. There were many servants in uniform. Now I could understand how zamindars and petty kings lived in the olden days.

Suresh came in two minutes. He was dressed in silk. He looked very pleased to see me. 'Welcome to our small abode. I am very happy you could make it. Let us go to the living room.'

His living room was full of statues, paintings, Persian carpets and chandeliers. There were silk-covered sofas made out of sandalwood. I felt I had entered a museum and not someone's home.

'Tell me Suresh, how you made your journey from college to this place.'

I remembered Suresh came from a very poor family. His father was a cook and had many children. He was unable to educate his son. A kind-hearted gentleman knew Suresh's father. He offered a room and food for Suresh in his own house. His son was also studying with us. Our college gave Suresh a full scholarship. We all knew his financial situation and we would help him in as many small ways as possible. We used to contribute money for him to buy books. Even the librarian went out of his way to give special concessions to him. Suresh was a fairly good student, hard working and very shy. He hardly spoke with us. So I wanted to know how he had become this affluent talkative Suresh.

'You know, after college I went to Bombay in search of a job. I got a small job. I worked very hard as I knew then that to come up in life you require talent, hard work, aggression and connections. I had the first two but had to build up the latter two qualities. Later I met Veena, my wife, whose father helped me a lot and we started a different business. Today I am well off. I helped out my family in various ways. You know I came from a poor family. I bought lands, shops, built houses which I gave to my parents, brothers and sisters. Everyone now owns two cars and is well off. I am very happy that I have done my duty towards my family.'

'What about your children?'

'I have two daughters. Both of them are studying in England, one is studying Indian culture and the other one is doing Home Science. Do you know any good boys who are well off and handsome for my daughters? But they should not want to stay with their parents. They must be either independent or live with us. You must be knowing some eligible men, you meet so many people.'

'Suresh, the people I meet are poor, helpless, destitute. Or I meet students. I don't know the kind of people you are talking about.'

By that time his wife called us for breakfast. The food was served in silver plates. Veena looked very beautiful and young. Only when she came near me I realized she was as old as I was. She had hidden her age with a lot of clever make-up.

Suddenly I remembered the gentleman with whom Suresh stayed, our college librarian, and the rest of the students in our college.

'Suresh, did you ever go to college after you left? Do you remember our librarian, the Principal, our batch mates?'

With a grim look on his face Suresh replied, 'No, I never went to college, nor have I met any one of them. Some classmates I have bumped into accidentally. I have invited them here. I never felt like going back to the college.'

'What about Mr. Rao? You stayed in his house, did you not meet him any time?'

'No. I feel everyone in college helped me because they wanted to feel better about themselves. After all I was a very good student. I am convinced people help others only with a selfish motive. They want to say, "I brought up a person". That is the reason why I never felt like meeting any one of them.'

Still I persisted, 'I heard Mr. Rao's financial condition is not good.'

Suresh replied emotionlessly, 'Yes, that was bound to happen. He fed so many unwanted students who were not good in studies or hard workers. How long could he continue like that?'

I remembered the institution which gave him free scholarship, the librarian who helped him, Mr. Rao who was his host for five years. They were all good, kind people but Suresh refused to recognize that. What was great about helping your own sisters and brothers? Giving them two cars and a few houses is not philanthropy. Helping somebody who is needy and without expecting anything from them in return is real philanthropy. In life, you must help others so that they can live independently.

Gratitude is the highest form of education, but Suresh never learnt that. Without receiving any help from others he could not have reached the position he was in that day. When climbing the ladder it is very easy to kick those below, but one must not forget that you cannot stay at the top forever. The higher you go, the longer is the fall.

I did not feel like eating breakfast from a silver plate that day.

In my Computer Science class, once I gave a very tough problem to my students. Programming is an art to some extent. When the same problem is given, different students use different methodologies to arrive at the same result.

I never insist on a single method and allow my students their freedom. This problem was very difficult and I myself took almost a week to solve it. When I brought my solution to class, my students wanted to check it. I gave my diskette to one of them, Nalini, and said, 'Please copy this program on your diskette and return mine. This is the only copy I have, so be careful.'

Everyone gathered around. Nalini inserted the diskette in the computer drive. While she was talking to me, by mistake she formatted the floppy. Formatting is nothing but clearing all the information on the diskette. Everybody was stunned. Then they looked at me. Nalini was in tears. They were aware that I had spent one whole week trying to find a solution to this problem.

For a while I was very upset. But after five minutes I cooled down and smiled. A smile can make tension disappear and is the best medicine in a friendship. After all my students are my young friends. When I smiled, the bubble of tension broke. I got up from my chair.

Nalini was sobbing 'Madam, I am very sorry. I did not do it purposely. Please forgive me.'

'I know you did not do it on purpose, Nalini. None of my students can do such a thing. Accidents do not require an invitation. Anybody can commit mistakes. If someone says he has never ever committed a mistake then he must be a robot, not a human being. Even our gods and our great rishis committed mistakes. Let us put our heads together and see if we can redo the program.'

Somebody asked me, 'Madam, how can you be so cool, when you have spent so much of time on that?'

'Yes, I am aware of it. I will somehow steal some time and try to write the program again. I am cool because I also committed a similar mistake when I was young.'

My students immediately switched the topic from Computer Science to storytelling. I told them my story.

'When I was young, I was very sensitive about what people said about girls. If they said "Girls cannot do that" immediately I used to feel I should do it just to prove them wrong. I wanted to show to the world that girls can do everything. Today I laugh at this logic. Men can do certain things well and women other things. Men and women are complementary to each other. One need not prove one's strength.

'That time, I was working in a computer software firm

as a system analyst. It was way back when computer hardware was not advanced. Today you have a tiny floppy of three and half inches. At my time a huge fifteen kg heavy Tandon Disc Drive was used.

'Casually my boss made a comment one day, "This disc is very heavy, only men can carry it."

'That remark upset me a lot. I told him, "I will carry it and show you."

'The disc was a bit like a gramophone but very heavy and large. It contained vital information of the company like its finances, employee details, etc. I took the disc and walked to the boss's room. It was really very heavy but I did not show it on my face. I believed strongly that showing emotions on your face is a sign of weakness. Today I feel one should be as transparent as possible.

'Seeing me walk in with the disc, my boss was surprised. "How did you manage to bring this?" he asked.

'Without thinking, in my happiness at having proved him wrong, I lifted my hand and left the disc.

'In a fraction of a second it fell and broke into pieces. The noise could be heard throughout the office. Everyone turned to look at me. It was the biggest mistake anyone had ever committed in the history of the company. It was an unforgivable error. The company's entire vital data was wiped out in a minute.

'I stood there dumbstruck. Because of my foolish behaviour the whole company was going to suffer. An employee should always work for the betterment of the company. But what had I done? I was so numb I could not even cry. I went back to my desk and sat quietly.

After thinking for a while I knew what I should do. I took a blank sheet of paper and wrote my resignation on it. That was the only way I felt I could atone for my mistake. I went to my boss's chamber and gave him the letter. Then I stood there, my head bowed in shame.

'He read the letter carefully. Then he tore it up. He said, "Everybody commits mistakes. I took a backup of the information on the disc before you lifted it. The data is still intact in the store room. You don't have to worry. Repentance itself is a punishment and you have repented enough. You should not be so sensitive. Sensitive people suffer a lot in life. Go and do your work."

'I did not have any words to say to him.'

Now I looked at Nalini and told her, 'It was also my mistake. I should have made a copy of such an important program. Please do not worry. I will rewrite the program. I still have some notes at home.

'That incident taught me that when you become a leader you should be kind and forgiving to your subordinates. It is not fear that binds you to your boss. Affection, openness and the appreciation of your qualities builds a long-lasting relationship. We spend most of our time at our work places. This time should be spent in happiness, not in blaming each other.'

My students broke into applause.

THE SECRET

In my class, about forty per cent of the students are girls and sixty per cent boys. When I studied Engineering thirty-five years back, I was the only girl in the course. I could only see boys and more boys everywhere. Today that trend has changed. People often ask me how I managed. But when I look back I feel it was not very difficult. Having a girl in the class was unusual for the boys, and initially I was the target for a lot of teasing. But over a period of time they became my best friends.

One day, in the class I was teaching, the students got into an argument. This happens often and I always allow them to speak. Normally this happens in the last class of the semester. I call it a free day, and there are no studies that day.

An argument had broken out between the girls and the boys about who was better. This is a very juicy topic and there is absolutely no end to the arguments. Suddenly the class was divided into two groups and the debate became emotionally charged. I sat back and enjoyed their arguments.

The girls said, 'It is ultimately the woman who makes the man. She is more powerful, has great endurance for pain and a better manager than a man. All successful men have been backed by supportive women. Without her help, man cannot achieve anything.'

The boys laughed at this, 'The woman will always be behind, never in the front. How many women have got the Nobel Prize? A woman's brain weighs less than a man's.'

I had to interfere here to say that there is absolutely no co-relation between the weight of the brain and its functions. The boys looked quite upset at my comment.

'Men start wars.'

'Wars happen because of women. Look at what happened because of Helen of Troy, Draupadi or Sita.'

The foolish arguments continued for a long time. Neither of the two groups was ready to accept the reality. Now I realized I had to step in.

I said, 'I will tell you a story. Listen to it and decide who is great.'

Immediately there was pin drop silence.

A long time ago there were two kings. One ruled over Kashi, and the other over Kosala. They did not like each other. Once both kings were travelling and they met. They were on their chariots. The road was small and only one chariot could pass at one time. Unfortunately, both chariots reached that spot at the same time. They stood facing each other. Which chariot would pass first? The kings refused to talk to each other, so their charioteers started talking.

The Kashi charioteer said, 'My king has ten thousand soldiers.'

The Kosala charioteer replied, 'My king also has ten thousand soldiers.'

'My king has two hundred elephants.'

'So does my king.'

'My king owns ten lakh acres of fertile land.'

'So does mine.'

The arguments carried on. It was very surprising that both kings had the same things.

Then the Kosala charioteer said, 'My king punishes bad people, dislikes lazy people and uses his money for the betterment of the kingdom.'

The Kashi charioteer replied, 'My king helps bad people become better human beings, makes a lazy person work hard and uses his money for the betterment of poor people.'

When the king of Kosala heard this, he told his charioteer, 'He is a better human being than me, I must become his friend. Give way to their chariot first.'

When the king of Kashi heard this, he got down and embraced the king of Kosala. Thus their enmity ended and they became friends.

I looked at my students and said, 'Today I will tell you a secret. I usually tell this at the end of the course in the last class. In real life, men and women are not opponents, they are the two wheels of a chariot. There is nothing good about one and bad about another. Both should possess good qualities.

'A person gets known by the qualities he or she possesses, not by the gender. That is decided by God.

'I am teaching you Computer Science today, but you will learn more in real life. Technology changes every day and good books are always there in the market. What I am teaching is also how to be a good human being. These values have not been prescribed in any syllabus nor will they appear in any examination. But these are the essential qualities you need, to do well in life. When you become older you should remember that there was a teacher who taught you the values of life along with your first knowledge of Computer Science. You must then teach your children these same values with as much love and affection.'

The class ended that day with my students gathered around me and all of us trying to hold back our tears.